Dear Clare . . .

. . . this is what women feel about Page 3

CLARE SHORT

Letters edited and selected by
Kiri Tunks & Diane Hutchinson

D1344478

HUTCHINSON RADIUS

London Sydney Auckland Johannesburg

© Introduction Clare Short 1991
© Editors' Preface Kiri Tunks & Diane Hutchinson 1991
© Selection Kiri Tunks & Diane Hutchinson 1991

The right of Kiri Tunks & Diane Hutchinson to be
identified as Editors of this work has been asserted
by Kiri Tunks & Diane Hutchinson in accordance with the
Copyright, Designs and Patents Act, 1988

This edition first published in 1991 by
Radius

Random Century Group Ltd
20 Vauxhall Bridge Road, London SW1V 2SA

Random Century Australia (Pty) Ltd
20 Alfred Street, Milsons Point, Sydney, NSW 2061, Australia

Random Century New Zealand Ltd
PO Box 337, Bergvlei, 2012, South Africa

British Library Cataloguing in Publication Data
Short, Clare
Dear Clare : this is what women feel about page 3.
1. Pornography. Portrayal by mass media
I. Title   II. Tunks, K.   III. Hutchinson, D.
364.174

ISBN 0–09–174915–8

Photoset in Plantin by Speedset Ltd, Ellesmere Port
Printed and bound in Great Britain

Contents

Acknowledgements

My thanks go to all the women who wrote to me, who moved me, made me laugh and educated me. I also thank the men who wrote, although their letters do not appear here. Special thanks go to the Editors of the letters, Kiri Tunks and Diane Hutchinson, for their meticulous work. I'd also like to thank Sam Chugg and many others in the Campaign Against Pornography for their work in the Off the Shelf campaign. Barbara Rogers and I have worked together for years on this issue and I have the greatest affection and respect for her.

There are special thanks for my wonderful mother, sisters and friends who helped to address the thousands of envelopes replying to the letters. And last, but not least, my thanks to my researcher, Virginia Heywood, who has typed hundreds if not thousands of replies. She is about to give birth to a daughter. Let us hope that she and other little girls will grow up in a better world that we can all help to make.

CLARE SHORT

We would like to thank the following for their help with this project: Colindale Newspapers Library; *Everywoman*; the Home Office; News International; National Childbirth Trust; the Press Council; the Three Hundred Group.

Our special thanks also go to Kit Allsopp; Andrew Bowyer; Vivien Green; Katherine McMurray; Kate Mosse; Tim Owers; Richard Russell; Clare Tester; Catherine Tidman; Sharon Tiernan; Andrew Wilson.

Finally, we would like to express our particular gratitude to Martha Street, whose support and assistance was invaluable.

KIRI TUNKS
DIANE HUTCHINSON

Illustration
Acknowledgements

"This processing plant is polluting the atmosphere! We must close down women immediately!"

We had hoped to reproduce several cartoons and columns, but *The Sun, The Star* and *The Sunday Sport* would not give us their permission to use anything in the book. We are, however, grateful to Express Newspapers for their kind permission to reproduce the above Cummings cartoon, 14 March 1986.

We would also like to express our grateful thanks to HMSO and the Editor of *Hansard* for allowing us to print Clare Short's Bill (p *xiii*) and the two Indecent Displays Debates (pages *xv* and *xxi*).

But the most important people to thank are all those women who were happy to let us print their letters – or parts of them – in this book. The publishers have tried in all cases to clear copyright, but in some cases this has not been possible. We would like to apologise in advance for any inconvenience this might cause.

Editors' Preface

We began this project in Spring 1989 as volunteers with the Campaign Against Pornography. At that time around 5000 letters that Clare Short had received after introducing her Bill were stored in boxes and it was suggested that the strength of feeling that these letters contained could – and should – form the basis of a book on the whole Page 3 issue. At the same time, Kate Mosse, at Radius, approached Clare Short suggesting that she should write her account of the various anti-pornography campaigns with which she has been involved since 1986. *Dear Clare . . .* is the combination of these two ideas.

For several months all we did was read and re-read the letters in order to familiarise ourselves with the points being raised and the different feelings this issue provoked in women. We then began to select individual letters, or parts of letters, which seemed to us to best present these various points and voices. Sometimes a single line effectively summarised what many women had said. As we worked, the letters themselves suggested several major themes which illustrated different facets of the same argument and showed how women themselves saw Page 3. Whilst the themes often overlapped – the central issue still being women's reactions to pornography – we thought that this method of organisation helped to unify the letters and give a coherent overall structure to the book. The issue was Page 3.

These letters are, for the most part, from women living and working in Britain. Many of the definitions and concepts here are the product of British culture which, while it does not exclude other cultures, doesn't necessarily represent them. The objectification of women is not singular to this country, but its methods do differ from place to place. The women who wrote were from all classes, of all professions and of all political persuasions. They had but one political axe to grind – theirs.

Many women asked us not to print their names and addresses. We have therefore only put the town of the writer in cases where this was indicated as being acceptable, just to illustrate how wide an appeal Clare Short's campaign had up and down the country.

A number of women began their letters 'I am not a feminist but. . .'. The word 'feminist' has been used by many sections of society as a term of abuse, implying man-hating, extremism, frigidity, prudery. Women hold views which object to their inequality and suggest solutions to it, yet they disown the term 'feminism' because they know the stigma that is attached to it and the way it is used to marginalise or dismiss the assertion of one's individual rights.

A book like this cries out for definitions. What is meant by the terms 'society', 'pornography', 'power', 'censorship'? The definitions are made clear by the way in which women have used these words. It is often very difficult for women expressing conceptual issues with man-made language. In order that women don't lose the thread of their argument by constantly having to define what *they* mean when they use a word, words like 'society' are used as shorthand for 'the society men have created'.

Similarly 'newspapers' or 'tabloids' are terms used in these letters when talking about the sensationalist or gutter press – the papers which rely regularly on the abuse of women through text and image to sell their news. There is no single word that adequately and specifically describes *The Sun*, *The Daily Mirror*, *The News of the World*, *The Sunday People*, *The Sunday Sport*, so although the use of these broad terms may at times appear careless there is no alternative. The use of the term 'men' may also appear careless but those that women attempt to describe are always some portion of this group. Definitions should evolve from usage.

There was a small proportion of letters that were written by men – less than 1% of the total. Some of these were supportive, but it was decided that no letters from men would be used in this anthology. This is a book about women's voices on an issue that affects them. It goes some small way to redressing the imbalance between male and female access to public expression.

The overwhelming message of the letters was one of support for what Clare Short was trying to do – make public and political an issue that for too long has been disregarded. The Page 3 and associated debates are old ones. We often hear from 'experts' but the real experts – the women who experience the effects of Page 3 – are rarely heard. They are the silent majority, because what they feel clashes so violently with what they are told. These women's voices are articulate and experienced but they are usually silent. Without representation there is no voice; without a voice there is no power. Many women found a voice on this issue. This is what they say.

Thank you on behalf of all those who are, and will be, silent.

TOWN WITHHELD

A
BILL

To make illegal the display of A.D. 1986
pictures of naked or partially
naked women in sexually provocative poses in newspapers.

B E IT ENACTED by the Queen's
most Excellent Majesty, by
and with the advice and consent of the Lords Spiritual and
Temporal, and Commons, in this
present Parliament assembled, and by
the authority of the same, as follows:—

1. It shall be an offence to publish in Offence and
newspapers pictures of naked or display of
partially naked women in sexually pictures of
provocative poses. naked women etc.

2. — (1) A person found guilty of an Penalties.
offence under section 1 above, shall be
liable on summary conviction or on
conviction on indictment to a fine not
exceeding one pence for each copy of
the newspaper published.

(2) A person found guilty on two or
more occasions of an offence under this
Act shall be liable to a fine not exceeding two pence for each copy of the
newspaper published.

3. For the purposes of this Act the Definition.
word "newspaper" shall mean any
paper containing public news and
published daily or on Sunday.

Indecent Displays (Newspapers)

12 March 1986

MS CLARE SHORT (Birmingham, Ladywood): I beg to move, that leave be given to bring in a Bill to make illegal the display of pictures of naked or partially naked women in sexually provocative poses in newspapers.

This is a simple but important measure. I stress that I should like the rule to apply to newspapers and only newspapers. If some men need or want such pictures, they should be free to buy appropriate magazines, but they have no right to foist them on the rest of us.

It is said that we are free not to buy such newspapers, but things are not as simple as that. I have received several letters from women whose husbands buy such newspapers. Those women object strongly to those newspapers and object to them being left lying around the house for their children to see.

I have also talked to teachers, including my brother. He asks children to bring newspapers to school for use in discussing current affairs or for making papier mâché, and so on. Both he and the children are embarrassed by the children's reaction to the Page 3 pictures.

A precedent for my Bill can be found in the Indecent Displays (Control) Act, which provides that public hoardings cannot show such pictures, although they are not illegal when they appear in magazines or when they are seen in private. The same reasoning applies: we should not all be forcibly exposed to them. The argument and precedent are exactly the same.

During the debate on the private Member's Bill introduced by the hon Member for Davyhulme (Mr Churchill), I said that I intended to introduce a Bill such as this. Since then I have received about 150 letters from all over the country. About one third of them are from men – *[Interruption]* – the vast majority of whom agree with me. Of course, I received some obscene letters from men, and Mr Murdoch and those Conservative Members who keep shouting out now should know that such people support and defend Page 3.

The letters came predominantly from women, particularly young women. They stressed time and again that they did not consider themselves to be prudes but objected very strongly to such pictures. One letter came from a young woman who worked in an office. She was writing on behalf of quite a few young women. They considered themselves to be young and attractive, but every day they were subjected to men reading such newspapers in the office, and to them tittering and laughing and, making rude remarks such as, 'Show us your Page 3s then'. Such women feel strongly that this Bill should be enacted. [*Laughter*]. Conservative Members display their attitudes for everyone to see, and will be judged accordingly.

Many of the letters that I received came from mothers with small children who said that they felt that page 3 undermined their efforts to instil decent attitudes in their children. Many of them commented time and again on the front-page stories of nasty newspapers such as *The Sun* – *[Interruption]*. It is the nastiest. Such stories deplore some brutal rape or attack on a child. The reader then turns to Page 3 to see the usual offering.

I agree with the women who think that there is some connection between the rising tide of sexual crime and Page 3. Obviously, that is unprovable, but the constant mass circulation of such pictures so that they are widely seen by children must influence sexual attitudes and the climate towards sexuality in our society. Those pictures portray women as objects of lust to be sniggered over and grabbed at, and do not portray sex as something that is tender and private.

When future generations read that in our day about 10 million newspapers carried such pictures every day to be left around and seen by children and by lots of women who did not want to see them, they will see those pictures as symbolic of our decadent society. That is why we should take action to make them illegal.

MR ROBERT ADLEY: (Christchurch): *rose —*

MR SPEAKER: Does the hon Gentleman seek to oppose the Bill?

MR ADLEY: Yes, Mr Speaker. The hon Member for Birmingham, Ladywood (Ms Short) is a prominent supporter of women's rights and her speech was a titillating mixture of politics, prejudice and prurience. It is barely credible that she should come before the House today with such a proposal. Why is she proposing that only pictures of women should be outlawed? Should we not outlaw cheesecake pictures of men? The hon Lady is clearly proposing to introduce a very sexist measure. Where are we supposed to draw the line?

Writing about her Bill in *The House Magazine*, the hon Lady refers to 'partially naked women in sexually provocative poses in *newspapers*'. The italics are hers, I imagine. It is fascinating to consider who will decide whether a woman is or is not partially naked, and whether her pose is or is not sexually provocative.

The hon Lady referred to *The Sun* and to Mr Murdoch. I noticed that she did not refer – it happened by sheer chance, I am sure – to *The Daily Mirror*. To make sure that I did my job properly in opposing the Bill, I had a look at *The Sun* and *The Daily Mirror* today. I am not sure which of these newspapers would fall foul of the hon Lady's strictures. Perhaps it is only newspapers owned by Australians, or perhaps by ex-Labour Members of Parliament who are now capitalists.

The hon Lady does less than justice to her fellow citizens. She would have our newspapers resembling *Pravda*. That would be more in keeping with some of her own political views. Where do we go from here? When the hon Lady has dealt with the newspapers and expunged from them everything that she finds objectionable, perhaps she and Mr Livingstone will go round the parks of London doing away with all the statues that she thinks might deprave people. There are a few pleasures left to us today. One that I enjoy is sitting in an underground train watching the faces of the people who are pretending not to be looking at Page 3 of the newspapers. If the hon Lady has her way, we will be deprived of that pleasure.

MR TONY MARLOW (Northampton, North): I believe that my hon Friend should treat this matter seriously, if only because I imagine that neither of us has ever seen the Press Gallery so full.

MR SPEAKER: Order. The hon Member must not interrupt. He knows perfectly well that there can be no interruptions of the debate on a Ten Minute Bill, and that, in any case, he must not refer to those who are not in the Chamber.

MR MARLOW: I apologise profusely, Mr Speaker.

MR ADLEY: The trouble with the hon Lady, and those who think like she does, is that she tends to mix only with those who share her views. To suggest seriously, as she does, that these pictures are offensive to the overwhelming majority of women is inaccurate. I suggest that they are offensive to the overwhelming majority of those with whom the hon Lady is in touch, which is not the same thing at all.

This is a ridiculous proposal. I propose to divide the House so that every Opposition Member can stand up and be counted. I suggested that, of all the measures that have been proposed to the House during this session, this Bill deserves the booby prize.

THE HOUSE DIVIDED: Ayes 97, Noes 56.

AYES

Alton, David
Ashley, Rt Hon Jack
Atkinson, N. (*Tottenham*)
Barron, Kevin
Beckett, Mrs Margaret
Beith, A.J.
Biggs-Davison, Sir John
Blair, Anthony
Boyes, Roland
Brown, R. (*N'c'tle-u-Tyne N*)
Bruce, Malcolm
Caborn, Richard
Campbell-Savours, Dale
Canavan, Dennis
Clarke, Thomas
Clay, Robert
Clelland, David Gordon
Clwyd, Mrs Ann
Corbett, Robin
Cox, Thomas (*Tooting*)
Craigen, J.M.
Cunliffe, Lawrence
Dalyell, Tam
Deakins, Eric
Dubs, Alfred
Duffy, A.E.P.
Dunwoody, Hon Mrs G.
Eastham, Ken
Edwards, Bob (*W'h'mpt'n SE*)
Evans, John (*St Helens N*)
Fisher, Mark
Foster, Derek
Freud, Clement
Godman, Dr Norman

Gould, Bryan
Hamilton, James (*M'well N*)
Harrison, Rt Hon Walter
Haynes, Frank
Hogg, N. (*C'nauld & Kilsyth*)
Holland, Stuart (*Vauxhall*)
Home Robertson, John
Howells, Geraint
Hoyle, Douglas
Hughes, Robert (*Aberdeen N*)
Hughes, Simon (*Southwark*)
Kennedy, Charles
Kirkwood, Archy
Lamond, James
Litherland, Robert
Lloyd, Tony (*Stretford*)
Lofthouse, Geoffrey
Loyden, Edward
McCurley, Mrs Anna
McTaggart, Robert
Madden, Max
Marek, Dr John
Mason, Rt Hon Roy
Maxton, John
Maynard, Miss Joan
Meadowcroft, Michael
Michie, William
Mikardo, Ian
Morris, Rt Hon A. (*W'shawe*)
Nellist, David
O'Brien, William
O'Neill, Martin
Park, George
Parry, Robert

Pavitt, Laurie
Pike, Peter
Porter, Barry
Powell, Raymond (*Ogmore*)
Rogers, Allan
Ross, Ernest (*Dundee W*)
Sedgemore, Brian
Short, Ms Clare (*Ladywood*)
Short, Mrs R (*W'hampt'n NE*)
Skeet, Sir Trevor
Skinner, Dennis
Smith, Cyril (*Rochdale*)
Spearing, Nigel
Squire, Robin
Steel, Rt Hon David
Stott, Roger
Strang, Gavin

Tapsell, Sir Peter
Taylor, Teddy (*S'end E*)
Thorne, Stan (*Preston*)
Thornton, Malcolm
Wallace, James
Wareing, Robert
Weetch, Ken
Welsh, Michael
Wigley, Dafydd
Wilson, Gordon
Winnick, David
Young, David (*Bolton SE*)

Tellers for the Ayes:
  Miss Jo Richardson and
  Mr Kevin McNamara

NOES

Adley, Robert
Atkinson, David (*B'm'th E*)
Baker, Nicholas (*Dorset N*)
Beaumont-Dark, Anthony
Best, Keith
Bevan, David Gilroy
Body, Sir Richard
Bowden, Gerald (*Dulwich*)
Brandon-Bravo, Martin
Brown, M. (*Brigg & Cl'thpes*)
Bruinvels, Peter
Buck, Sir Antony
Cocks, Rt Hon M. (*Bristol S*)
Coombs, Simon
Dicks, Terry
Dover, Den
Dykes, Hugh
Emery, Sir Pete
Fairbairn, Nicholas
Faulds, Andrew
Fletcher, Alexander
Forsyth, Michael (*Stirling*)
Fox, Marcus
Fry, Peter
Gardiner, George (*Reigate*)
Grylls, Michael
Hamilton, Neil (*Tatton*)

Harris, David
Hayward, Robert
Jessel, Toby
Jones, Gwilym (*Cardiff N*)
Jones, Robert (*Herts W*)
Kellett-Bowman, Mrs Elaine
King, Roger (*B'ham N'field*)
Latham, Michael
Lawrence, Ivan
Leigh, Edward (*Gainsbor'gh*)
Lightbrown, David
Lloyd, Ian (*Havant*)
McCrindle, Robert
MacKay, Andrew (*Berkshire*)
McQuarrie, Albert
Miscampbell, Norman
Mitchell, Austin (*G't Grimsby*)
Nelson, Anthony
Nicholls, Patrick
Norris, Steven
Ottaway, Richard
Peacock, Mrs Elizabeth
Shepherd, Colin (*Hereford*)
Silvester, Fred
Smith, Tim (*Beaconsfield*)
Stern, Michael
Stewart, Andrew (*Sherwood*)

Temple-Morris, Peter   Tellers for the Noes:
Wiggin, Jerry   Mrs Edwina Currie and
                                  Mr Greg Knight.

Question accordingly agreed to. Bill ordered to be brought in by Ms
Clare Short, Ms Jo Richardson, Miss Joan Maynard, Mrs Ann
Clwyd, Mrs Anna McCurley, Mrs Renée Short, Miss Betty
Boothroyd, Dame Judith Hart, Mrs Margaret Beckett and Mrs
Gwyneth Dunwoody.

INDECENT DISPLAYS (NEWSPAPERS)

Ms Clare Short accordingly presented a Bill to make illegal the
display of pictures of naked or partially naked women in sexually
provocative poses in newspapers: And the same was read the First
time: and ordered to be read a Second time upon Friday 18 April
and to be printed.

Indecent Displays (Newspapers)

13 April 1988

MS CLARE SHORT (Birmingham, Ladywood): I beg to move, that leave be given to bring in a Bill to make illegal the display of pictures of naked or partially naked women in sexually provocative poses in newspapers.

The purpose of the Bill is to remove from newspapers pictures of partially naked or naked women in sexually provocative poses and to make the publication of such pictures punishable with a fine relating to the newspaper's circulation. The proposal follows closely the principle of the Indecent Display (Control) Act 1981, which lays down that pictures that might legally be allowed in magazines cannot be put on public hoardings. I believe that the same argument should apply to newspapers.

I first introduced this Bill two years ago and you will recall, Mr Speaker, that on that occasion the House – particularly a large rump of Conservative Members – misbehaved fairly grossly. With some Conservative support, we won the vote on that occasion, but the Bill failed because a succession of Conservative Members objected each time that it came up for Second Reading. They did not even have the guts to stand up and say who they were but objected anonymously.

I seek to reintroduce the Bill, partly because of the overwhelming support that the proposal has received since it was introduced. I have received more than 5000 letters, the overwhelming majority from women but a significant number from men, supporting the proposal. Some of the letters are very moving and distressing. I have received about 12 from women who have been raped and who say that when they were raped the men said that they reminded them of a woman on Page 3 or that they ought to be on Page 3.

I have received many letters from women who were sexually assaulted and who say that every time they are exposed to such pictures it reminds them of the assault and they find it extremely distressing. I have received hundreds of letters from women who speak about sitting on a bus or the tube or being at work and seeing men reading papers and making comments that offend them deeply. I have received letters from women who have had breasts removed because of cancer and who are deeply hurt when sometimes even their husbands buy newspapers and bring them into the home.

I have received hundreds of letters from teachers who talk about children being asked to bring newspapers into school to cover desks during art lessons. They talk of little boys of six and seven giggling and joking over the pictures while the little girls do not know what to do. That is some indication of the way in which such newspapers are helping to shape attitudes in our society.

The last category of letters, and perhaps the most upsetting, concerned those from young women who were sexually abused as children and who talk about the way in which the man who abused them, often the father or a close relative, used such pictures and pornography to justify the sexual abuse.

The overwhelming majority of those who write argue that the pictures degrade women and portray them as sexual objects to be used and taken whenever men feel the need to do so. It is the overwhelming view of those who wrote to me, and it is also my view, that the mass circulation of these pictures – we are talking about 10 million every day of every week of every year and about twice that number of adults and large numbers of children who see them – helps to create a sexual culture that encourages sexual assaults on women and rape and sexual abuse on women and children.

The wide distribution of such pictures helps to legitimise the harder and nastier porn, the circulation of which is also growing rapidly in our society. Some of those who oppose my Bill argue that they have some sympathy for it but that it would be wrong to censor the press. I should like to address that argument. The British press is owned by a very small number of extremely rich men. It seems quite extraordinary to suggest that that small number of people can define freedom while the rest of us are not allowed to impose some constraints on what they print and circulate. Quite rightly, we have restrictions on material that excites racial hatred. We should also have restrictions on material that degrades women.

It is far from certain that the readers of these newspapers want the pictures. Every easy-to-read newspaper in Britain carries such pictures, but only one of them, *The Star*, has ever consulted its readers. The majority of those who bought the paper and responded to the poll said that they wanted the pictures to be removed. The last time that I introduced my Bill it was followed by a campaign in one of our lowest level newspapers, *The Sun*, which wanted to stop 'Crazy Clare' from introducing the Bill. Readers were asked to send for car stickers and to write using Freepost to say how they objected to the Bill. Ever since that time *The Sun* has refused to tell anyone how many stickers were circulated and how many people wrote in.

A small number of dirty-minded newspaper owners and editors who despise their readers think that they have to serve up such material in order to sell some of their nasty politics. It is not the wish of the people who buy the newspapers that such material should be widely circulated in our society.

I hope very much that the House will overwhelmingly support this measure. I do not pretend that it will prevent all sexual attacks on women or stop the degradation of women. However, it would be one big step in that direction, and the House should be united in supporting it.

MR ERIC FORTH (Mid-Worcestershire): This is an intolerant measure and is typical of the authoritarianism we have seen in the modern Labour Party. In this I have some sympathy with the right hon Member for Chesterfield (Mr Benn), because I am beginning to understand what he is saying about this trait in the modern Labour party.

This measure sits ill with the Opposition's criticisms about the censorship of the press, the authoritarian attitude of Government Members or the Government's attitude towards the press. I hope that Opposition Members will think carefully about that before they vote on this measure.

What upsets Opposition Members is that this matter is about choice. It is about the choice exercised freely every day by millions of people. As the hon Member for Birmingham, Ladywood (Ms Short) has admitted, millions of people in this country exercise their choice freely to purchase newspapers and to look, among other things, at whatever may be displayed in them.

Perhaps more importantly, it is about the choice made by the young ladies themselves as to whether they display themselves in the newspapers. I wonder what it is that the hon Member for Ladywood finds so objectionable about adult young ladies deciding whether they will exploit the audience for those newspapers. She has talked about the exploitation of them, but I wonder whether she had considered how successfully young ladies choose to display for profit whatever assets they possess and benefit and exploit the male population of this country. It may well be that she is wishing to protect the wrong people.

What distinction is made between the honourable place of the nude in the history of art and sculpture and the portrayal – [*Interruption.*]

MR SPEAKER: Order. We often hear things in the Chamber with which we may disagree.

MR FORTH: What distinction –

MR BRIAN SEDGEMORE (Hackney, South and Shoreditch): Name one painting.

MR FORTH: For the benefit of the House I will name the sculpture 'The Kiss' by Rodin, which is generally accepted as a great work of art and which portrays two naked people in an embrace.

MR SEDGEMORE: Name one painting.

MR FORTH: Why is it that the prurient minds of Opposition Members see unclad young ladies as being disgusting? [*Interruption.*]

MR SPEAKER: Order. I am listening with great interest to what is being said, but I cannot hear properly if there are interruptions from below the Gangway.

MR FORTH: I would cite further the works of Titian or Reubens and many other great artists who have portrayed through the centuries ladies in various stages of undress whose pictures have been regarded as art.

The Bill is defective in its detail – [*Interruption.*] I do not know why Opposition Members are afraid to hear the argument. Perhaps they are embarrassed by what their hon Friend is proposing.

MR SEDGEMORE: What Titian painting is the hon Gentleman talking about?

MR FORTH: Will the hon Gentleman settle down?

MR SPEAKER: Order. All I can hear from below the Gangway is some chant about a painting. This Bill is about displays in newspapers.

MR FORTH: The measure is defective in its detail because the hon Member for Ladywood failed to tell us who will define what is meant by 'partially clad'. Who decides between clad, partially clad or unclad? More importantly, and perhaps more relevant, what is a sexually provocative pose? Perhaps the hon Lady can identify or knows a sexually provocative pose when she sees one, but I do not know whether she expects the readers, editors or publishers of the newspapers so to do. She has not described in the Bill where the responsibility for the identification of 'partially clad' or 'sexually provocative' will lie.

This is a grossly irresponsible and defective measure, and, for all those reasons, I hope that the House will reject it. It is intolerant and impractical and flies in the face of the freely exercised choice of most people in this country.

THE HOUSE DIVIDED: Ayes 163, Noes 48.

AYES

Abbott, Ms Diane
Allen, Graham
Alton, David
Ashton, Joe
Banks, Tony (*Newham NW*)
Barnes, Harry (*Derbyshire NE*)
Barron, Kevin
Beckett, Margaret
Beggs, Roy
Beith, A. J.
Bell, Stuart
Benn, Rt Hon Tony
Bennett, A. F. (*D'nt'n & R'dish*)
Bidwell, Sydney
Boyes, Roland
Bradley, Keith
Braine, Rt Hon Sir Bernard
Bray, Dr Jeremy
Brazier, Julian
Brown, Gordon (*D'mline E*)
Brown, Nicholas (*Newcastle E*)
Bruce, Malcolm (*Gordon*)
Buckley, George J.
Butler, Chris
Caborn, Richard
Callaghan, Jim
Campbell, Menzies (*Fife NE*)
Campbell, Ron (*Blyth Valley*)
Campbell-Savours, D.N.
Canavan, Dennis
Clark, Dr David (*S Shields*)
Clay, Bob
Clelland, David
Cohen, Harry
Cook, Robin (*Livingston*)
Corbyn, Jeremy
Cormack, Patrick
Cousins, Jim
Crowther, Stan
Cummings, John
Cunliffe, Lawrence
Dalyell, Tam
Darling, Alistair
Davies, Ron (*Caerphilly*)
Dobson, Frank
Doran, Frank
Duffy, A. E. P.
Dunnachie, Jimmy
Dunwoody, Hon Mrs Gwyneth
Eadie, Alexander

Eastham, Ken
Ewing, Mrs Margaret (*Moray*)
Fatchett, Derek
Field, Frank (*Birkenhead*)
Fields, Terry (*L'pool B G'n*)
Flynn, Paul
Foot, Rt Hon Michael
Forsythe, Clifford (*Antrim S*)
Foster, Derek
Fraser, John
Galbraith, Sam
Garreth, John (*Norwich South*)
Gould, Bryan
Graham, Thomas
Grant, Bernie (*Tottenham*)
Griffiths, Nigel (*Edinburgh S*)
Grocott, Bruce
Hardy, Peter
Hattersley, Rt Hon Roy
Haynes, Frank
Heffer, Eric S.
Henderson, Doug
Hinchliffe, David
Hogg, N. (*C'nauld & Kilsyth*)
Home Robertson, John
Hood, Jimmy
Howarth, George (*Knowsley N*)
Hoyle, Doug
Hughes, John (*Coventry NE*)
Hughes, Robert (*Aberdeen N*)
Hughes, Robert G. (*Harrow W*)
Illsley, Eric
Janner, Greville
Jones, Barry (*Alyn & Deeside*)
Jones, Martyn (*Clwyd S W*)
Kilfedder, James
Kinnock, Rt Hon Neil
Kirkwood, Archy
Lambie, David
Lamond, James
Leighton, Ron
Lewis, Terry
Litherland, Robert
Livingstone, Ken
Livsey, Richard
Lofthouse, Geoffrey
Loyden, Eddie
McAllion, John

McAvoy, Thomas
McCartney, Ian
McFall, John
McKay, Allen (*Barnsley West*)
McKelvey, William
Madden, Max
Mahon, Mrs Alice
Marek, Dr John
Marlow, Tony
Martin, Michael J. (*Springburn*)
Martlew, Eric
Maxton, John
Meacher, Michael
Michael, Alun
Michie, Bill (*Sheffield Heeley*)
Michie, Mrs Ray (*Arg'l & Bute*)
Milan, Rt Hon Bruce
Moonie, Dr Lewis
Morgan, Rhodri
Morley, Elliott
Mowlam, Marjorie
Mullin, Chris
Nellist, Dave
Nicholson, Emma (*Devon West*)
Oakes, Rt Hon Gordon
O'Brien, William
Orme, Rt Hon Stanley
Parry, Robert
Patchett, Terry
Pike, Peter L.
Radice, Giles
Redmond, Martin
Rhodes James, Robert
Rooker, Jeff
Ross, Ernie (*Dundee W*)
Rossi, Sir Hugh
Rowlands, Ted
Ruddock, Joan
Sedgemore, Brian
Sheldon, Rt Hon Robert
Shephard, Mrs G. (*Norfolk SW*)
Short, Clare
Skinner, Dennis
Smith, Andrew (*Oxford E*)
Smith, C. (*Isl'ton & F'bury*)
Smith, Rt Hon J. (*Monk'ds E*)
Spearing, Nigel
Squire, Robin

Strang, Gavin
Straw, Jack
Tapsell, Sir Peter
Taylor, Mrs Ann (*Dewsbury*)
Thomas, Dr Dafydd Elis
Turner, Dennis
Vaz, Keith
Wall, Pat
Wallace, James
Wareing, Robert N.
Welsh, Andrew (*Angus E*)

Welsh, Michael (*Doncaster N*)
Widdecombe, Ann
Williams, Alan W. (*Carm'then*)
Wilson, Brian
Winnick, David
Worthington, Tony

Tellers for the Ayes:
  Mrs Ann Clwyd and
  Ms Jo Richardson.

NOES

Adley, Robert
Alexander, Richard
Arnold, Jacques (*Gravesham*)
Atkinson, David
Banks, Robert (*Harrogate*)
Beaumont-Dark, Anthony
Biggs-Davison, Sir John
Blackburn, Dr John G.
Brittan, Rt Hon Leon
Budgen, Nicholas
Butterfill, John
Carlisle, John (*Luton N*)
Carttiss, Michael
Coombs, Anthony (*Wyre F'rest*)
Coombs, Simon (*Swindon*)
Couchman, James
Day, Stephen
Emery, Sir Peter
Farr, Sir John
Fearn, Ronald
Fox, Sir Marcus
Goodson-Wickes, Dr Charles
Gow, Ian
Gregory, Conal
Grylls, Michael
Haselhurst, Alan

Heathcoat-Amory, David
Hicks, Mrs Maureen (*Wolv' NE*)
Holt, Richard
Jessel, Toby
Johnston, Sir Russell
Jones, Robert B (*Herts W*)
Kirkhope, Timothy
Lawrence, Ivan
MacKay, Andrew (*E Berkshire*)
Moate, Roger
Oppenheim, Phillip
Paice, James
Redwood, John
Riddick, Graham
Shaw, David (*Dover*)
Shaw, Sir Michael (*Scarb'*)
Stewart, Allan (*Eastwood*)
Taylor, Ian (*Esher*)
Tebbit, Rt Hon Norman
Warren, Kenneth
Whitney, Ray
Wiggin, Jerry

Tellers for the Noes:
  Mr Eric Forth and
  Mr Jerry Hayes

Question accordingly agreed to. Bill ordered to be brought in by Ms Clare Short, Ms Jo Richardson, Mrs Margaret Beckett, Mrs Alice Mahon, Mrs Ann Clwyd, Mr John Battle, Mr Bill Michie, Mrs Ann Taylor, Mrs Margaret Ewing, Ms Diane Abbott, Ms Marjorie Mowlam and Miss Emma Nicholson.

INDECENT DISPLAYS (NEWSPAPERS)

Ms Clare Short accordingly presented a Bill to make illegal the display of pictures of naked or partially naked women in sexually provocative poses in newspapers: And the same was read the First time: and ordered to be read a Second time upon 6 May and to be printed.

Introduction

The story of how I came to introduce my Page 3 Bill is, I think, worth telling, not least because it all really came about by accident. This does not mean that it was trivial or unimportant. But all I did was to voice in the House of Commons the revulsion most women feel at the mass distribution of pornography in the tabloid press. Partly as a result of the misbehaviour of many male MPs, the issue was drawn to public attention. It was the reaction of thousands of women throughout the country that made the debate significant. I was simply a woman in Parliament who felt as other women do. Together we caused quite a storm.

It all began, I suppose, when I was elected to the House of Commons in 1983, as Labour MP for Birmingham, Ladywood. There are many rooms around the building where there are racks containing all the national newspapers. For most of us it is the first time we have been so much in the public eye, and therefore we are ruthlessly scrutinised. Naturally when the press are attacking you for something – and it usually is an attack – you look to see what they are saying. It also means that you see papers that you've never really concentrated on before. It was this experience that made me flinch at the surprisingly large number that contained full page photographs of women in poses which really say take me, use me, throw me away. I was also struck by how often the front page story covered a nasty rape or a vile attack on a child: the headlines screamed denunciation, but then I turned over to Page 3 and felt that they were hypocrites. There was almost a sense that the reporting of such attacks was intended to be sexually titillating. I felt a deep sense of revulsion, but like most women I simply turned away and left it behind me, thinking there was nothing I could do.

Then one Friday at the beginning of 1986 I had to cancel all my weekend engagements in order to stay in the House of Commons to help block Enoch Powell's Bill, which would have made treatment illegal for couples with infertility problems. Friday is normally allocated to Private Members' business – either Bills or

Debates. If you have no particular interest in the subject, those MPs with out-of-London seats rush off to their constituencies, because Friday is the only weekday available to visit schools and other organisations that are shut over the weekend. I felt very strongly that Enoch Powell's Bill should be opposed. The effect of the Bill would have been to prevent any experimental work on embryos. If it had passed it would have meant that many couples that desperately wanted a child would not be helped. Current practise allowed such work up to 14 days of age of an embryo (at this stage the embryo is no bigger than a full stop on this page). I felt strongly that experimental work should be allowed to continue. So rather than being on a train to Birmingham, that Friday afternoon found me still in the Commons.

Nothing, of course, is straightforward in the House of Commons. We had already had a debate on the Powell Bill, but in order to prevent it from being further considered we had to ensure a long debate on the preceding Bill, since there is not normally time to consider more than one Bill fully in an afternoon. The Bill under discussion had been introduced by Winston Churchill, Tory MP for Davyhulme, and was intended to change the law on Obscene Publications. It was a terrible Bill. It listed a series of images that would be treated as obscene whenever and wherever they were printed, a list which included scenes of horrific violence as well as various descriptions of sexual activity. Its effect would have been to outlaw most war reporting, many illustrations in medical textbooks and much sex education material. As a result of publicity about the Bill, I remember that I received letters from a group involved in sex education for mentally disabled young people, which pleaded with us to prevent the Bill from passing because they found it essential to use pictures and the Bill would have made their work illegal. The Bill later fell apart in Committee and never had a real chance of becoming law. But the very nature of the debate on the Bill made me very irritated indeed.

I sat in the Chamber of the House of Commons for several hours listening to speech after speech. There were speeches on the grave danger of the Bill with which I entirely agreed. There were also many comments – largely from the Conservative benches – saying that women throughout the country were increasingly angry about the threat of sexual attack and would never forgive the House of Commons if it did not pass the Bill.

I had not prepared a speech but was stirred by all this misleading argument to get up and speak. I said that it was true that women were angry about the threat of sexual violence but that did not mean that they would support such a ridiculous set of proposals. And having voiced my agreement with those who had spoken about the grave dangers of the Bill, I added that if the House of Commons really wished to respond to women's anger, we should introduce a Bill to remove Page 3 pornography from the press. This would be tightly drawn, would not endanger any other freedom, but would be an important step in removing the widespread circulation of degrading images of women in our society. And that would be a real step towards addressing women's fears. As I spoke, I got carried along and I ended up by saying that I would consider introducing my own Bill to this effect.

It was quite late in the day by this time and the press gallery was virtually empty and my speech was not widely reported. But it must have been covered in some local newspapers, because the following Monday morning I started to receive letters from women saying they thought my proposal was brilliant and asking me please to go ahead with it. So, because of a chance, unplanned House of Commons speech, I found that I had struck a chord with women everywhere. It was decided that I would introduce my Bill.

There are two procedures for Private Members' Bills. Most legislation is introduced by the Government. The Opposition has no opportunity to introduce legislation. Individual backbench MPs of all parties get a chance once in every Parliamentary session to enter a ballot and the top ten or so are given time on Fridays to introduce their Bills. The only alternative is a 10 Minute Rule Bill, where you get the chance to speak for 10 minutes on your Bill on a Tuesday or Wednesday. Another Member can oppose if he or she wishes and call a vote. If you win the vote, you have permission to bring in the Bill. It then goes to the back of the queue for Private Members' Bills – that is, after the top ten in the original ballot – which means you rarely have time to take it further. But it can be a good way of raising new issues and putting proposals before the House of Commons and the country.

There is a peculiar procedure for obtaining permission to bring in a 10 Minute Rule Bill. There is a room, high above the Chamber of the Commons, where you go to queue. If you are the first there on certain appointed days, you win permission to bring in your Bill. Once I went to the room at 6 am and then again 4 am, but each time found an MP sitting in the armchair before me. I therefore decided in February 1986 to camp out with a sleeping bag to ensure I was first in the queue. I arrived at about 1 am, and slept comfortably on the floor until I was awakened by a cleaner making worried noises. I asked her sleepily whether she wasn't used to MPs queuing up for Bills. She said she was, but they were usually men in suits sitting in the armchair not women in green dresses lying on the floor! But I had at last succeeded in obtaining the time for my Bill.

The appointed day came round three weeks later, 12 March 1986. But rather than excitement, I felt sadness. The day before I had been called out of Committee on the Wages Bill where I was leading for the Labour Party in opposition to Government proposals to reduce legal minimum protection for low-paid workers. The message said my father had died. My father lived with me and I went home immediately. He was 83 and had been very ill, but he was a very fine man and it was a terrible loss. My mother, brothers and sisters and I sat up late that night comforting each other. I contemplated dropping my Bill, but decided not. I had promised it to many people and it had taken much time and effort to get the chance. It seemed a better tribute to my father to carry on, rather than to give in.

The House was quite full because 10 Minute Rule Bills come up before the main business of the day. As I spoke, putting the case for the removal of pornographic pictures from the press, a large clump of Tory MPs began to giggle and chortle and make crude remarks about me, my Bill and my body. I had not prepared for the Bill by asking Labour MPs to be there, but there were a considerable number and as I was attacked they supported me. Robert Adley, Tory MP for Christchurch, spoke in opposition to my Bill. He made what many will think was a silly, juvenile attack that he obviously thought very funny and then it came to the vote.* Two Labour MPs voted against and one of them, Austin Mitchell, told me afterwards that he faced more attacks for this than most other things he had done in his political life. I am not attempting to suggest by this account that all Labour men are perfect and the Tories terrible, not least because I am sure that some of their support can be explained simply by loyalty to a Member of their own party. I had sought support from women on all sides of the House for the Bill. Only one Tory woman, Anna McCurley, who was then MP for Greenock and Port Glasgow, gave her support. Edwina Curry, Tory MP for Derbyshire South, took a different view. She attacked the Bill and acted as a teller for the opposition. She even commented to the press that her husband wished she looked like the pictures – her husband later denied this. The vote was 97 in favour, 56 against. I had won permission to bring in my Bill.

* You can judge for yourself how silly his contribution was on p *xvi*

The press the next day continued to try to belittle me and my Bill, with the usual sexual innuendo and ugly photos. The parliamentary sketches in the so-called 'quality' papers were as dismissive as the tabloids. Having skimmed the press, I went to the post office to pick up my post in my usual way. I always receive a big bundle of mail but this day was exceptional. The bundle was massive. I hurried to my desk wondering what the letters would say. What I found were hundreds of loving, caring, supportive letters from women. They sent me pictures of their daughters and cards with beautiful pictures of flowers. They wrote to say how much they agreed with me. But the most urgent message was that they were shaking with rage at how I was treated. I was deeply touched by this enormous affection from women I had never met. The strength and loveliness of it far outweighed the humiliation and nastiness I had experienced before.

As the days went by, the letters continued to flow in. They came in their thousands. They were enormously welcome but created real problems for me just in opening and reading them and sorting them from the letters from constituents that urgently needed my help with immediate problems. I involved my mother and sisters in helping me open and sort the mail. I also had to decide how I could possibly reply. It was impossible to write individually to each. I prepared a standard letter and organised my family and friends sitting round on the floor at weekends stuffing replies into envelopes and helping to address them.

Not only was I deeply moved by the letters, but I was educated too. They said so much, so eloquently. Women of all ages, backgrounds, politics and experiences wrote about their feelings. Some brought me to tears. I remember especially an early letter from a young woman who said she had been raped some time ago. She had blamed herself ever since. But she said that when she heard me say that many women believed that there was a link between the mass circulation of such images and the rape and sexual abuse of women, she had realised for the first time that the attack was not her fault. This meant a lot to her because throughout the rape the man had kept saying that she ought to be on Page 3. She thanked me and said she felt much better. There were letters from women who had had breasts removed in cancer operations, who said how much it hurt them that their husbands brought such papers into their house. I remember one who asked me not to write back because her husband would be angry if he knew she had written to me.

There were lots of letters which said 'I am not a feminist or I didn't think I was' but went on to argue vehemently against the damage and insult caused by pornography. Hundreds of women told me how they had hated the pictures for years but never dared to object because they would be accused of being jealous. They said how happy they were to find out that other women felt as they did.

After a few weeks, *The Guardian* diary ran a small piece, after picking up gossip around the Commons that I was receiving vast numbers of letters. They rang, and during the course of the conversation I mentioned how very few of the letters had been from men. I then received hundreds of letters from men apologising. Many of them said how completely they had changed their views about Page 3 when they had sons and daughters of their own and began to think about the world that they were growing up in.

Amongst all this warmth there was, of course, an ugly side. There were maybe 50 or 60 envelopes containing pornographic pictures with my head glued on to replace the original, with obscene threats scrawled across them saying that I should be quiet and go away because I was only jealous because I was too ugly to rape. I found these distressing, but also interesting: in their own nasty minds, these men were making a direct connection between pornography and rape.

The Sun newspaper took a particularly virulent line in their attacks on me. They branded me 'Crazy Clare', 'Killjoy Clare', and assembled a number of unflattering photographs and printed them daily inviting their readers to write in Freepost to 'Stop Crazy Clare'. They also produced a car sticker and invited readers to send for one. I've only ever met one person who has seen the sticker, Jeremy Corbyn, Labour MP for Islington North. When a number of journalists later enquired how many readers had written in, *The Sun* refused to answer. They also refused to say how many car stickers had been distributed.

Shortly after my Bill was introduced, *The Sun* approached a number of MPs who had voted against me asking them to appear on Page 3 with their favourite 'lovely'. Four or five did this, including Peter Bruinvels, then Tory MP for Leicester East, and a member of the Church of England Synod. I received another letter from the chair of one of their Conservative Associations saying that she had demanded an apology from her MP, Geoffrey Dickens, who hadn't been present to vote but had agreed to appear on Page 3. The apology was duly given. Another interesting example of women's power.

The Sun did cause me one panic attack. I didn't, of course, read the paper and didn't bother to look at it properly when their hate campaign was on. But one evening I received a phone call from one of my sisters who lives in Brighton. She had met a friend in her local pub who told her he'd seen a copy of *The Sun* at work. There was a piece entitled 'Twenty Things You Never Knew About Crazy Clare'. It was impossible for me to see a copy of the paper until I went to the House of Commons library the next day; I thought and worried about all the things I had ever done in my life in which *The Sun* might be interested. When I finally saw the piece, I laughed with relief. They listed such 'horrifying' accusations as that I had once appeared at the despatch box in tight black trousers and a long pink jacket; that I was supposed to be left wing but right wingers in the Labour Party said they liked me; and that I had been a Civil Servant . . . *The Sun* continued its campaign for years. During the 1987 election, they printed a completely blank Page 3 with a little box saying this is how their paper could be if 'Killjoy Clare's' party won the election.

The Star behaved rather differently. Joe Ashton, Labour MP for Bassetlaw, first ran a piece disagreeing with me the day after I presented my Bill, but then voted in favour two years later. The women's editor, Alix Palmer, who had been initially hostile to my Bill, had a similar change of mind. She looked back through the Page 3 pictures and noticed how, over the years, they had become more suggestive and the captions more crude. In July 1987 she wrote a piece saying that she had changed her mind, she thought that the pictures did degrade women and should be removed from the paper. I was then telephoned at home and told that *The Star* had decided to consult its readers on their attitudes to porn in their paper by organising a computer phone-in. I was asked if I welcomed this and said of course I did. To myself, I had a little worry. The readers did, after all, buy the paper. Would they support me? But the result of the poll was that an overwhelming majority of women said that they wanted the pictures taken out. A small majority of men wanted to keep them. So, the overall finding was that a majority of *The Star* readers who bothered to phone the Freephone, wanted the pictures removed. The editor, wrote a piece saying that he found this very interesting and would have to think about it, but nothing changed. Some months later, however, it linked up with *The Sunday Sport* and seemed to move further downmarket and carry more porn. They also ran a story about how a 15-year-old girl was assaulted by a man on her way home from school and suggested this was because her breasts were so large. In the story, it claimed she said she had liked it when her attacker stuck his tongue in her mouth. On a TV programme about the link up between the two papers she said this was a complete lie, she had never said such a thing and had hated the attack. *The Star* later disentangled itself from *The Sunday Sport*. Interestingly Tesco and the Co-op had withdrawn their advertising. Advertising for shopping is aimed at women and both retailers probably judged that the new *The Star* would offend women and therefore was not the place for them to advertise. This is another interesting example of women's power once they start to make their views known.

Many women have written to me objecting strongly to the revolting *The Sport* and *The Sunday Sport*. These so-called newspapers were launched by one of the most well known pornographers in Britain, David Sullivan. It is said that he concluded that there was more money in newspapers that carry porn than in specialist pornography magazines. The paper is ridiculous as well as revolting. It carries headlines such as 'I was pregnant for 64 years and gave birth to a pensioner', or 'Revealed, Hitler was a woman'. It also carries lots of pornography, advertisements for sex lines and stories that glamorise gang rape and other abuse. On 9 October 1986 I spoke at a CPBF meeting in Manchester with the original editor of *The Sunday Sport*, Michael Gabbon. He quickly alienated the audience. When asked by a man whether he would cease to publish if it could be shown that pornography caused rape, he answered that it would depend on how many rapes. The man said 'say it was 6'. His answer was 'that isn't very many'.

The anger of the women that write is that this publication lies amongst the newspapers to be looked at by children when it should at the very least be on the top shelf. In 1988 when the paper first appeared the National Union of Journalists ran a campaign called 'Shelve It' calling for it to be confined to the top shelf. I understand that the Press Council recommends that it should be placed on the top shelf. But in practice nothing happens. My answer to those who write is that if I could only get my Bill passed, the paper would have to close. In the meantime, I suspect it would be worthwhile starting to make complaints to the police. There is a law forbidding indecent displays, and in my opinion the front cover of *The Sport* is frequently indecent. I imagine the prosecution of a number of newsagents would soon result in the removal of *The Sport* to the top shelf, which is at least a start.

Anyway, as the months rolled on and the letters continued to pour in, there started to be a turn-around in media coverage. A number of women's magazines, such as *Woman* and *Cosmopolitan*, covered the issue and consulted their readers about their views. Overwhelmingly women expressed agreement with the proposal.

On 25 March 1986 I raised the issue with Mrs Thatcher at Prime Minister's Question Time. I had all along genuinely believed that the issue was one for women and not for party politics. The reaction had from the start been different between the two parties, although there had always been a minority on the Tory benches that supported me. Mrs Thatcher was dismissive in her reply. I found all of this very odd. In the past, it had been Tory MPs that had tended to support Mrs Whitehouse and her campaigns. I was critical of her approach because she tended to favour a widespread censorship that would endanger basic freedoms. But I had assumed that when I introduced my tightly-drawn Bill, there would be cross-party agreement. This was not forthcoming – with some honourable exceptions. I found out later that Robert Adley sent out a letter to his critics defending himself, saying that the Bill had all been a ploy on my part to attack *The Sun* because of the dispute at Wapping. This was misleading. In fact I had extended my criticism and the effects of my Bill to all the papers that carried porn. This included *The Daily Mirror* – a paper that tends to support the Labour Party, though at the time in a rather half-hearted way. The truth is that *The Sun* had celebrated its Page 3 more brazenly than other papers. It was also true that it had attacked me more viciously than other papers. But I had hoped to appeal to all women, of all political persuasions and none. I had even hoped this might include Mrs Thatcher. But I was forced to conclude that Tories felt they had to oppose me because *The Sun* supported their politics.

While all this was happening outside the House of Commons, I still had to organise things inside Parliament. Once the principle of the Bill had been passed, I was required to draw up the detail in order to have it printed. I was anxious to draw the Bill very tightly, since I did not want it to have ridiculous, unintended effects such as, for example, outlawing pictures of olympic swimmers or pictures explaining to women how they should examine their breasts to prevent cancer. I therefore made it an offence to print pictures of 'naked or partially naked women in sexually provocative poses in newspapers'. I did not wish anyone to be imprisoned for the offence and therefore made the penalty a fine of 1p per copy circulated. I was conscious that Page 3 was only produced to make money, and therefore thought the penalty should be financial. The effect of this would also be that if some small, local paper was stupid enough to print pornographic pictures, the penalty would be in proportion to their means.

Following the passage of the principle and the printing of the Bill, it was necessary to obtain a date for its consideration. It is very difficult to get 10 Minute Rule Bills passed because any one Member of the House can simply shout 'object' and constantly have it put back to a later date until the current session of Parliament comes to an end and the Bill dies. So I knew that it would be very difficult but hoped that after all the furore over the Bill, no one would dare to object. The dates for consideration are always on a Friday, so it meant giving up more of my precious Fridays in Ladywood. On each occasion a Tory backbencher shouted 'object'. They did so very quickly and were careful not to identify themselves. It is interesting that on many Bills, the whips representing the official position of the Government shout out 'object' from the front bench. I got the distinct impression that Government whips made sure that there was opposition to my Bill but preferred it to come from the backbenches so that the Government would not be embarrassed, in being seen to object to a Bill which clearly had widespread public support. This pantomime continued over a number of Fridays until the parliamentary session ended in June and the Bill quietly died. Its death was celebrated by *The Sun* placing five partially-naked women on Page 3 with remarks about what I should do with myself.

Letters continued to arrive throughout 1987 in a steady stream. Groups of women in various places organised petitions and sent them to me. I have never known an issue like it. I received five thousand letters before I stopped counting. On many issues, powerful organisations encourage individuals to write to their MPs. We all receive many letters when such campaigns are on, but they rarely number more than hundreds. On this issue, where no powerful lobby had asked anyone to write, thousands of women put pen to paper to express their views and fears. It is precisely because I wish to share the importance of these letters that this book is being published. Of course the letters are printed anonymously but the women concerned have all been consulted. I am only sorry that some of the most powerful and moving are not included. Some of them were so intimate and self revelatory that I thought it right to destroy them immediately after I replied. I regret this now. I suspect that many of the women concerned would have liked to share their views and experiences. But at the time, this book had not been thought of and I judged it more responsible not to keep these letters. Nevertheless, I believe the selection contained here does give voice to the eloquence and depth of feeling of women on this issue. That is the importance of this book – it gives voice to the strongly-held views of women who are rarely given a platform from which to speak.

After a year or so, I began to receive letters asking what had happened to my Bill and pleading with me not to give up. By coincidence I found that I came tenth in the ballot for Private Members' Bills in November 1987. I knew it was unlikely that the Bill would pass on the second occasion when it had been so strongly opposed on the first, but I felt I could not let all those women down by introducing a different Bill. I felt that they would think that I had given in. This time I added to the Bill a clause making it illegal to display pornography in workplaces, an issue on which I had also received many letters. On 13 April 1988 when my Bill was introduced for the second time, the atmosphere in the House of Commons was very different. It was deeply charged, the press gallery was full to overflowing and Tory whips scuttled around ensuring that there was less crude behaviour on this occasion. They obviously judged that the previous behaviour had damaged their image. To me, this seemed to indicate the way in which we were beginning to win the argument. Eric Forth MP opposed the Bill on this occasion. He was shortly afterwards made a Minister in the Department of Trade. The vote was 163 in favour, 48 against, an increased majority. The coverage in the press was not sympathetic but was toned down compared to the previous occasion. Another indication that we were beginning to win.

After introducing my Bill however, I became concerned that there was no constructive outlet for the strength of women's feelings, apart from writing to MPs. I had therefore joined up with others to try to launch a campaign against pornography. It is not easy to get a new organisation off the ground, to obtain funding, an office and staff, but we managed to do this in a small way. CAP obtained some financial support from the Cadbury Trust to help subsidise the monthly feminist magazine *Every-woman's* publication of 'Pornography and Sexual Violence – Evidence of the Links'. This was simply a record of the evidence presented in Minneappolis in December 1983, when the state legislature was considering bringing in a Bill to tighten the law on pornography. It was significant because it summarised a large body of evidence – some academic, some from individuals who had worked in the porn industry and some from those who had been damaged by its effects. Despite this being American not British research, the level and availability of pornography is similar in both countries, and in the absence of adequate research here, we felt strongly that such information should be made available. I do not believe that we should be required to prove academically that pornography is degrading and objectionable in order to voice opposition. But I do believe that it is significant that so few women are aware of the research referred to in the Minneapolis hearing that demonstrates that male college students exposed to pornography for a period of time are more likely to say that they would rape a woman if they could get away with it.

We considered launching a campaign to encourage newsagents not to stock porn and, when successful, inviting local women to patronise the porn-free shop, which would be awarded a sticker. But like all good ideas, this had occurred to someone else. The Christian organisation CARE had started just such a campaign and had great success in some parts of the country. Interestingly, after the second introduction of my Bill, a number of newsagents contacted me, said they had decided to cease stocking porn and said that they had experienced an increase in their sales.

I think that there is room for much greater progress with this idea. When you think about it, we have newsagents in every small shopping area throughout the country. This is where we all go to buy our papers and children go to buy their comics and sweets. Almost every one of them has a top shelf full of porn. This reflects the massive quantity of pornography which is distributed and sold in Britain and the fact that it is considered mainstream and acceptable. In the United States of America, the figures have been added up. Their pornography industry is larger than the film and record industries combined. I am sure that it is equally large in Britain. We live in a society saturated with pornographic images of women.

This was the thinking behind the Off the Shelf Campaign, launched by the Campaign Against Pornography and supported by the National Union of Students and the Townswomen's Guild. The campaign was co-ordinated by our hard-working volunteer Sam Chugg. We decided that we should seek to challenge the top shelves full of porn in local newsagents and invite women to use their voices and buying power to object. We picked out W. H. Smiths as our first target, not because we had any animus against W. H. Smiths in particular, but because they were a large, supposedly respectable high street retailer that claimed to have a social conscience and tends to set standards for the industry as a whole. Smiths is also a major wholesaler stocking even more porn than it sells in its shops, and so carries a large part of the responsibility for the mass distribution of pornographic material in Britain.

Having made preparations for the Off the Shelf Campaign launch in January 1990 we called a press conference and, followed by TV cameras, swept into the Kingsway branch of W. H. Smiths in London. We took all the porn down from the shelves, dumped it by the cash till and explained our objections. We invited groups of women throughout the country to do likewise and they did. Others wrote to their local W. H. Smiths manager saying they would not shop with them in future. One granny – as she called herself – from Wales wrote to me in great glee to tell me how she had filled up her basket with goods, waited in a long queue, then after the items had been rung up asked if her branch of W. H Smiths stocked porn. When she was told they did, she refused to pay for the goods and caused mayhem.

The campaign went well and there were actions all over the country. W. H. Smiths became quite worried, and invited us to meet their Chairman of Directors, to discuss the campaign. Our representatives were told that if we could produce evidence to show that pornography was linked with sexual violence, Smiths would reconsider their position. Of course we didn't have the resources to undertake the sort of research that would have been acceptable to them, so until some larger group receives funding for this crucial work, we will have to hope that public opinion becomes so overwhelming that they will be forced to change their policy. But I do not think that we should be despondent. A lot has already been achieved. Retailers and distributors are feeling increasingly defensive and women increasingly confident about objecting to porn. I hope that local campaigns will continue to encourage at least one local newsagent to get rid of their top shelf of pornography and that women will ensure with their purchasing power that porn-free newsagents prosper. I also hope that women everywhere will keep up the pressure on W. H. Smiths and that it will eventually be forced to change its policy.

Dawn Primarolo, Labour MP for Bristol South, and the Campaign for Press and Broadcasting Freedom have been involved in another important campaign to challenge the mass distribution of pornography in newsagents. Dawn introduced a Bill, of which I was a sponsor, to require that pornography be sold only from licensed sex shops. I do have some reservations about the proposal because there is a problem with sex shops. We have one in Ladywood which is near a major church and a number of banks. The church and the banks have joined together to get the place closed down because, in the case of the banks, their staff – who are largely women – are constantly accosted by men visiting the sex shop. A neat proposal was put to me in June 1990 by Robin Corbett, who is a fellow Birmingham MP. He suggested that we should legislate to require porn to be sold only by mail order. This would mean no one who didn't want to see it would have to, and those who did want it would have to make special efforts to find it. The fact that it was not openly displayed would reduce its legitimacy and respectability. I also suspect that many women would be astonished to find it turning up in their letter box and that this would take the argument further as men who think it quite acceptable to consume porn found out what the women in their lives thought about it.

I should make it clear that I am not advocating solutions that simply sweep all pornography under the carpet, but allow it to continue to prosper. There is no quick legislative fix available that will suddenly cause pornography to disappear. I look forward to the day when those who produce it and use it are treated as furtive outcasts rather than just as 'one of the lads'. But in a society where pornography is mainstream and respectable, we have to find ways of unleashing women's power to object and thus push it further and further back until it disappears altogether. No one should forget that the law is applied by policemen, and sometimes policewomen, magistrates and juries that are part of the main-stream of society. Parliament will not pass nor society uphold legislation which seeks to impose standards that have not won the consent and support of the mainstream. Thus it is important for us to challenge the acceptablility of pornography in the main-stream, so that we can shift the public awareness of the degradation of women that it breeds.

Another issue that hits my mail bag is the widespread advertisement of sex lines. Since the telephone system was privatised in 1988 these lines have proliferated. I am told that the lines are basically teasers, trying to keep men talking as their phone bills mount up, and always promising much more later. But as the advertisements proliferate, women are offended and objections are raised. I find it very depressing that so many men would be attracted by all of this and that women – often poor women with few other options – should be employed to do it. My colleague Terry Lewis, Labour MP for Worsley, has campaigned long and hard to tighten up the regulations of this sordid business.

There are few in Britain who dare to deny the unacceptability of child pornography, though I was recently approached at a meeting by a man who tried to persuade me it was harmless. But when we look into the links between child pornography and child sex abuse I believe that there are lessons to be learned about all forms of pornography. Some of my letters came from women who had been sexually abused as children. They talked about the use of pornographic pictures by their abusers to suggest that what was being done to them was quite normal. They also talked of how such images hurt, upset and reminded them of their childhood experiences when they were confronted with them in their daily lives.

The law in Britain is very firm on child pornography. But paedophiles continue to collect and produce it. Early in 1990, I visited the unit that deals with illegal pornography at New Scotland Yard, a visit that had been arranged by Ray Wyre of the Gracewell Clinic in Birmingham, who felt that MPs should be more aware of police activities in this area and the difficulties they faced. The police showed me a video compilation of the kind of illegal pornography with which they have to deal, warning that I might find it upsetting. I was haunted by some of the images for a time – a little girl of about 4 being urinated over, a boy of 9 being sexually abused, his face showing his confusion and hurt. There were also shots of women being mutilated in an enormously gross way, fingers being chopped off – even intestines ripped out and severed in the course of sexual encounters. There were fairly obvious fakes, but the question is why should such ugly and vile acts give sexual pleasure? The main concern of the police officers concerned was child pornography. They argued that whenever it was found, child sexual abuse was also to be found. They were concerned that through lack of resources they were unable to follow all the leads that became available to them and thus were failing to prevent abuse to children. It says something significant about the values of our society that such a unit is under-resourced.

Tim Tate recently produced a book on child pornography.* I think it is a valuable book which should be widely read and acted upon. But I also think he is wrong to suggest – as some others do – that child pornography is the only problem and that we should not be concerned about other forms of pornography. Some seem to feel that the issue is simply about protecting those who cannot protect themselves, namely children. But the truth is that one kind of pornography too easily slips into another. The Page 3 girl in a gymslip may be over 16, but the imagery is clearly intended to present schoolgirls as sexual objects. There are pornographers who specialise in choosing over-age women who look very young and then showing them and projecting them as childlike. Of

*Child Pornography – An Investigation, Methuen 1990.

course child pornography must be dealt with with the utmost priority. But I believe there is a continuum. The presentation of children or women as powerless sexual objects to be taken and used against their will, often with violence, is the real issue. The presence of such images, like it or not, does help to legitimise abuse.

Over the last 3 or 4 years, I have taken a serious interest in the question of child abuse. It began with a therapist in Birmingham raising it with me when I spoke at the AGM of the Rape Crisis Centre on pornography in 1986. I told her that I would like to help, but needed educating. I followed the question in the press and had knowledge of my own childhood experiences – as it seems all women do, when we come to talk – but did not consider myself sufficiently expert to make public pronouncements. She organised a briefing for me and sent me reading lists. I came across a number of cases in my constituency Advice Bureau. I went through the emotions of revulsion and anger as I read and understood more. Now people are perhaps more aware of the horrifying extent of the problem, but then it was still a taboo subject. I ended up feeling most angry with those who wish to deny that there is a problem and those in authority who ignore it and chose to do nothing about it. I came to know Ray Wyre after we first met on a *Call Nick Ross* programme on rape on Radio 4 in late 1986. I was deeply impressed with his understanding and expertise, and his belief that there was a clear link in our culture between the widespread distribution of pornography and the abuse of women and children. This view was not the result of academic research, but of his work with rapists and child abusers as a probation officer and now a therapist at the Gracewell Clinic. The clinic attempts, with considerable success, to treat such men, understand what causes them to act as they do and to prevent them acting in this way again.

At the Gracewell Clinic I met men who have been convicted of horrific abuse of children. They come in all shapes and sizes and are not the mad strangers beloved of the tabloid press. Child abusers come from all classes and backgrounds. Some are highly educated and successful in their careers. Many of them have been abused as children. But even this does not explain it, since some who are abused go on to abuse, but others do not. Ray Wyre is convinced that the widespread distribution of pornography helps them to believe that their behaviour is normal and acceptable, that if we wish to prevent such abuse, we must denounce all such imagery of sex. He tells me that the minority of rapists and child abusers who are convicted are allowed to fester in prison, often sharing pornography, and thus reinforce in each other the belief that they are normal and have been mistreated.

I feel that the refusal of our system to seek to examine, treat and learn from those who engage in such offences is a form of collusion. If we really wish to prevent rape and the sexual abuse of children, surely we would study all the evidence available and make the necessary changes to try to prevent the offence as well as punishing the offenders? I am pleased that the Home Office is beginning to take this argument seriously, with the announcement in December 1990 that sex offenders are to be provided with treatment in a new experimental programme, but there is a long way to go.

There is another example of this problem. A probation officer, Monika Sabar, wrote to me in 1989 to say that she had come across cases where detailed statements about rape cases were being circulated in prisons as a form of pornography. *The Guardian* also ran a piece on 27 June 1990 about this disturbing trend. I discussed it at the Gracewell Clinic with a man just released from prison for a child sex abuse conviction. He said that paedophiles also swapped their prosecution statements in return for tobacco as a form of pornography. The response from John Patten, Minister of State at the Home Office, explained carefully why he would not take action. I then requested a meeting in August 1989 and he promised to do more. Attempts are now being made to remove the names and addresses from such statements and more action is promised. John Patten has said that he wishes to try to deal with the problem through administrative action before considering legislation.

An aspect of police reaction to pornography was brought to my attention by letters I received. One young woman told me that she went to a police station in London to report a sexual attack and was confronted by a pornographic calendar. She went home feeling sick. She did not report the attack and felt that she could not trust the police who proudly displayed it on their wall. Another woman went with her small daughter to report a road accident and was confronted by a similar calendar. Both asked me to take action. Receiving no satisfaction from the Home Office, who said it was a matter for each force, I wrote to each Chief Constable in Britain to ask their attitude to the display of pornography in police stations. Some said they took a strong view, others said they had no idea and some said they would make enquiries. Shortly after this my car broke down on the way to Bridlington. The police were helpful and took me to a part-time station to ring the AA. Above the phone I found what had clearly been a pornographic calendar with the pictures torn off. I hoped this was the result of my survey. Many women solicitors have told me stories of what they find when they are let in behind the counter. It seems to me that it is totally unacceptable and painful to think of women going to police stations to report a sexual attack and being confronted with a display of pornography.

It is time now for me to bring my introductory remarks to the letters to a conclusion. Before doing so, I think it is important to try to answer some of our critics. There are some standard arguments that are trotted out to try to silence women who dare to object to pornography. In this introduction I have simply attempted to tell the story of my engagement with the issue. *Dear Clare* . . . is not supposed to be a book on every aspect of pornography, nor a history of the various debates that have taken place on the question. For me this has just been one small part of the work I do as an MP. But I have learned so much from the letters and the places to which the subject has led me, that I simply wish to share my experiences with others. Those who read this book may well not have had any involvement with anti-pornography campaigns or equally may be experts. So I'm going to address – briefly – some of the standard objections that are most frequently thrown in to any debate about pornography.

The first is the definition of pornography; who is to decide what is pornographic and what erotic? Conceptually, it is easy to distinguish between what we mean by pornography and pictures of nakedness and acceptable sexual imagery. Pornography degrades and belittles women and depicts them as permanently available to anyone. Erotica depicts attractive pictures of nakedness and sexuality which suggests mutuality and respect and sensuousness. We all know the difference when we see it. Those who feel the need to defend pornography may argue about the distinction but all of us recognise the difference in the concept and the difference in reality.

It is suggested that those of us who object to pornography are embarrassed about sexuality and nakedness. That we are against sexual pleasure and screwed up about our own sexuality. Norman Tebbit put this argument very crudely in answer to mine, suggesting in *The Spectator* in May 1986 that Page 3 in the tabloid press was the working class version of pictures of naked women in art galleries throughout the world. Eric Forth, opposing my Bill in 1988, also tried to follow this line but was unable to substantiate the argument. My simple answer is that the difference between pornography and nakedness is the same as the difference between child pornography and the pictures that exist of most of us, as naked babies, in family albums throughout the land. There is obviously nothing wrong and ugly about nakedness, just as there is nothing more wonderful than mutual, sexual relationships. But nakedness and genuine sexual relationships are very different from the constant proliferation of pictures of women in poses with captions which say, take me, use me, dispose of me. As soon as the pictures move from the newspapers to the top shelf, the legs are splayed and shortly thereafter come the whips and boots and – frequently and significantly – Nazi regalia. And it is now a well-documented fact that Nazis did actually use pornographic pictures of their perceived enemies with the aim of reducing respect for them in the outside world – if you like, dehumanising them. It was, as we know, a successful tactic. All such pictures are about using women for sexual pleasure without mutuality, frequently with associations of violence and power. Each and every one of us knows the difference whenever we see such pictures.

Some letters made the point in a different way. They wrote to say that they agreed with me, but that women had no chance of being afforded dignity by the owners and editors of the tabloid press. They suggested instead that we demand equal treatment. This would entail equal numbers of pictures of men who should be equally revealed. They rejected adamantly the idea of the male pin-up that parts of the press have tried to push. A man in boxer shorts or a towel is in no way equivalent to a picture of a woman with breasts revealed in a provocative pose. They suggested that pictures of men with their genitals fully revealed and crude headlines about the size of their genitalia would produce instant demands from all men for the removal of the pictures. I would not dream of making the argument on the grounds of taste, not to mention not wanting to be involved in extending the level of degrading images printed in the press. But the question they pose is why there are so many such pictures of women and not of men. Clearly the issue is not nakedness.

Some letters talked of the unnaturalness of the pictures themselves. Ex-models wrote to me about how much they regretted having done it. (Current fashion models wrote about their resentment about the pressure they were under to remove their clothes.) The models told me about the ridiculous antics that went into the pictures – buckets of ice beforehand to swell their breasts and nipples, Sellotape to make them look more erect than they were. They described hilariously the convolutions that went into the poses. They were very clear that these were simply not 'natural' poses.

One very honest man said to me at a CPBF meeting on pornography at the 1990 Labour Party Conference that he was happy to have learned about good sex from a number of good women in his life. He said however that when he was a young man he was both scared of and fascinated by sex and that he had considered pornography to be his sex education. I think this very interesting and suspect it is true of many men. Men have written to say that pornography does not just degrade women but also degrades men. They talk of the pressure they feel under to join in and pretend they like it. The group at work huddling round the newspaper suggesting what they would like to do to the woman depicted. I think that all of this is connected with sexual insecurity. Men want to prove to each other that they know about and are good at sex. But many of them are deeply worried about it.

I read a very interesting article some months ago in *The Sunday Times* magazine written by a woman who taught sex eduacation in schools. She argued that much had changed for girls. Women had become more secure about their sexuality and had reached out to their daughters and pupils to try to talk honestly about sex and menstruation and growing bodies in a way that our grandmothers had often failed to do. But she felt that boys were being left out of the process. Mothers naturally felt a growing physical distance and sexual restraint as their sons became adolescent. Most men found it difficult to talk about sexual relationships, be they fathers or teachers. She argued that boys were left very much on their own with their changing bodies and sexual feelings and worries about appropriate behaviour. I suspect that there is a lot of truth in this and thus boys look to the tabloid press and the pornographers to try to learn about women's bodies and sexual behaviour. We must begin to attend to a better education of our young men about their sexuality. It would, I am sure, make them happier and the women in their lives happier. It would also, I suspect, reduce the consumption of pornography. My conclusion on this is that it is hopelessly sad to think of many men using pornography for sex education. I do not know how widespread it is, but I suspect the honest man at the CPBF meeting said something very important. If it is true that this use of pornography is widespread among men. I think it perhaps helps to explain why so many relationships between men and women are badly screwed up.

There is a lobby that is deeply hostile to my arguments on the grounds that in opposing pornography we are being hostile to gay people. They suggest that any law against pornography will inevitably be used against gay literature. I must confess that I can see absolutely no way in which my Page 3 Bill would ever be used in any way to penalise gay literature, but I do not think this is the point of the argument. The suggestion is that any criticism of expressions of sexuality will be used against gay sexuality, but surely this argument is as illogical as the case made that opposition to pornography is actually opposition to sex itself?

I have received a number of letters from gay men and lesbians who support my case and argue that pornography is about degrading sexuality. I also received a copy of a very interesting draft article from a gay man that argued that gay expressions of sexuality had been so repressed that it was an act of defiance and liberation to produce gay pornography. He went on to argue that when this phase was over, gay men could afford to question this depiction of their sexuality and would begin to object to degrading imagery, but that this stage had not been reached.

For myself, I must admit that I know little about gay pornography but should considerations of sexual morality apply only to heterosexual relationships? Clearly the same standards that expect human beings to treat each other with respect and not to impose cruel and vicious sexual exploitation on each other apply to gay and lesbian people as much as to heterosexual people. So I would say that pornographic – rather than erotic – depictions of gay sexuality must be as unacceptable as heterosexual pornography. A young man who gave evidence to the Minneapolis hearings on pornography said that he was gay and had for some time lived with a man who bought large quantities of violent gay pornography and expected him to act out the depictions. He said that this was oppressive and ugly and that he objected to it. This seems to me to be an exact equivalent of my understanding of the degradation of violent heterosexual pornography.

I answer these arguments simply because they are so frequently put. My concern with pornography is the degradation of women. I will do all I can to oppose the repression of gay people because I believe in human dignity and civilised behaviour, whilst completely rejecting the suggestion that women objecting to pornography are in any way involved in attacking gay people. Sexual dignity and self confidence and lack of degradation must lead to more civilised attitudes towards everyone.

Another criticism often levelled is that women not only choose to buy papers such as *The Sun*, *The Star* and *The Daily Mirror*, but that women appear in pornography and make a lot of money out of pornography and therefore criticism of pornography is an attack on women. I appeared once on Kilroy Silk's programme when he was discussing pornography. The programme had assembled a group of young women who were either working in the porn industry or wished to do so. Some of them had brought parents or boyfriends with them, the idea clearly being to set up a conflict between me and these young women. I found this very sad. I had refused all previous requests from programme makers to appear against women who pose for pornography. Some – a very small minority – of my letters had argued that the problem arose because these 'bad' women agreed to pose and thus let down their own sex. This is not my view. Those who control and distribute pornography are men, usually rich men. They use young women for their pictures and then dispose of them when they begin to age. A few well-known figures make money, but the majority of young women who are drawn into this industry find themselves in an ugly, sordid world that lives side by side with prostitution.

On the Kilroy Silk programme, there were a number of good looking young women, or women with large breasts, from backgrounds that offered little chance in life, who had dreams of becoming Samantha Fox. I felt no criticism of them, just sadness. This was the one opportunity they felt that our culture offered to them. It was a lesson in their powerlessness and the distortions of our culture. In 1986 one of the tabloids – the Agony Aunt being another Claire – actually published a letter where 'Dear Claire' said that she couldn't advise a young hopeful to become a Page 3 girl, and that she 'wouldn't have it on my conscience'. And this from a paper with a daily pin-up. . . .

At last I come to the argument about censorship. The word censorship is clearly such a bad word, symbolising lack of freedom and the prevention of honest discussion that many people simply throw it into the argument and think that it is enough. They feel that in the face of such a powerful word, we should all simply fall silent and go away. There is a sense, paradoxically, in which the word is used in order to censor debate. Women start to talk about their objection to pornography, the word censorship is produced and that is supposed to end debate.

It seems to me that we should disentangle two arguments. The first is about the nature of pornography. Is it beneficial or harmful? Does it degrade women? Does it generate a widespread attitude that women are available to be taken and used and disposed of? Does it encourage men to think little of women? Does it define women as sex objects and disentangle their sexuality from their brains and personality so that they have to struggle to be both a woman and a person? Do many women dislike it? Do many women feel belittled by it? I think that the answer to all these questions is yes, and that most women agree. If this is all true, we have to ask why is there so much of it? Who produces it? Who consumes it? Who makes money out of it? Why is it such a big business?

When we have discussed all these things, we have to ask what we should do about it. As I have said, it seems to me that those who instantly cry censorship want to stop us even from talking about this first set of questions, let alone begin to ask what we should do.

Once we have demanded the freedom to discuss pornography and why we dislike it and why it circulates so widely, we can ask what we should do. But at this stage in the argument we have to examine what freedom is. Is freedom what Maxwell and Murdoch choose to put in the press? Must we allow, in the name of freedom, all three big conglomerates headed by three very rich men to determine what our press is like? Don't the rest of us have a right to impose some restrictions on these rich men? There are few people now who believe that it is wrong to have a law making it an offence to incite racial hatred. Most people would agree that this is an enlargement rather than a restriction of freedom.

There are few people who argue publicly that there should be no restrictions on child pornography. But if the present law is right, is it censorship or a protection of children's freedom? There are those who have been critical of my arguments who do not call for a repeal of the present laws on obscenity. Why is this right? How can anyone possibly suggest that any tampering with the present law is censorship?

It seems to me that if these powerful and important words – freedom and censorship – are used so lazily and hazily, then those who are using them are not protecting freedom but actually doing the opposite and defending pornography. I do believe, however, that the powerful emotions women feel about pornography must not be allowed to be used to legitimise dangerous measures that would endanger real political and artistic freedom. It is my view that many of the campaigns mounted by people like Mary Whitehouse in the past have done just that. I have spoken with Mary Whitehouse once only. I was at the time working in the Home Office as Private Secretary to Mark Carlisle, the Minister of State with among other things responsibility for Obscene Publications. I was about 25 at the time. Mary Whitehouse telephoned my office one day and demanded to speak to my Minister. I explained that he was not available and offered to take a message. She said that she had been to see a film and wanted Mr Carlisle to prevent it being shown. She then went on to describe in meticulous detail what she found objectionable about the film. I squirmed with embarrassment as I made notes of what she said. She said repeatedly that I must tell Mr Carlisle in full detail everything she had said. I did not do this of course. I passed on the message, said that she objected to sexual scenes in the film and wanted him to ban it. He dealt with it from then on, but as he said, she knew as well as he did that he did not have the power to ban the film. Later on I went to see it. It was called *Blow Out* and was about a group of French people eating themselves to death. It was weird and wonderful and the sex was incidental.

I noticed that she was later reported as saying that the Vietnam war should not have been reported in the way it was in the USA because 'it undermined the will of American youth to fight' and making similar criticisms of the reporting of the South African war in Namibia. For me the suggestion that a war should not be reported thus preventing the people of a country deciding whether it was a just war is a terrifying diminution of freedom. This is censorship.

Winston Churchill's laundry list Bill – which started me on the road to my Page 3 Bill – would have had the same censoring effect. The Bill was strongly backed by Mary Whitehouse. There was a later Obscene Publications Bill introduced by Gerald Howarth which I opposed because it was similarly widely drawn. I argued in the Committee on the Bill that because it sought to outlaw factual scenes of horrific violence that would shock reasonable people it was deeply dangerous. I took the example of the little girl in Vietnam who had been napalm bombed and ran naked down a road – a photograph that moved the world. This was clearly a scene of horrific violence that would shock and outrage reasonable people. One of the Tory MPs argued that there would be no harm in such a picture being lost. Again, this is censorship.

My own view is that it is the failure of the Left, of libertarians and those who wish to protect human dignity to deal with the issue of pornography that has allowed those who favour dangerous censorship to misuse the emotion women feel about pornography. The answer is not to ignore the question of pornography and be intimidated by the accusations of censorship, but to define what is bad in it. To be clear that we do not agree with those who believe that all sex is bad and should be confined to the minimum necessary to procreate within marriage. That we do not accept censorship of war reporting or medical textbooks but that we do object to the belittling of women and thus to the degradation of sexuality.

Alongside this debate about the nature of pornography and the liberation that challenging it brings, comes the power to use women's voices and purchasing power to object to it and push it backwards. And thus we get advertisers reviewing their material and the motor-show ceasing to use naked women sprawled across the bonnets of cars. This was the purpose of the Off the Shelf campaign. It was not a legislative proposal, but a campaign involving all women and inviting them to take on the largest retailer in the country to warn them that we would take our custom elsewhere if they continued to stock porn.

And finally, I also favour tightly drawn legislative proposals that would remove pornography from the press without endangering any other freedom. And thus we would use the power of democracy to impose some standards of civilisation on the mighty barons who own our press and believe that they can damage women's dignity and freedom with impunity. We are also entitled to review the existing Obscene Publications Act to see if we could create a better legislative framework. But we must always remember that we are acting in the name of freedom and human dignity and we must not support any proposal that would endanger precious freedoms in the name of our dignity. We must not allow our real agenda to be distorted.

Closely aligned to the censorship lobby are those who seem to believe themselves entitled to lay down what everyone else should think. They do not want a broad-based campaign, however it might benefit other women, and will not allow anyone to agree with them unless they agree with everything they think. Thus I have received a few letters from women who were upset because they were not allowed to sign the CAP petition supporting Off the Shelf. One of the local activists knew they were opposed to abortion so would not allow them to be opposed to pornography. We had similar problems at a conference CAP arranged in Nottingham in connection with the Off the Shelf campaign. When it began, all women MPs had been circulated and asked for their support. One of those who agreed to give it was Jill Knight, the Tory MP for Birmingham Edgbaston. Some of those at the conference criticised us viciously for publicising the fact that she supported the campaign, the reason being that she had been a supporter of Clause 28 and had unprogressive views on race and immigration. I'm in favour of abortion, opposed to Clause 28 and do not feel that I have anything in common with those on the so-called Hard Right who would like pornography banned. But then neither do I think I have anything in common with pornographers, the press barons who oppose the banning of Page 3 on the grounds of their reduced profits. You can't choose your causes on the basis of people's views on other subjects. I condemn apartheid, another MP in favour of the Poll Tax also condemns apartheid –that doesn't make me rethink my position on apartheid just because I disagree with them on this other issue.

I am deeply opposed to this purist mentality. I favour a broad-based movement of all women to challenge porn wherever we find it. We can continue to argue over the other questions. But if our cause is good, I see no problem in seeking support everywhere. If this helps us to enhance the dignity of women, it can only be good. There is also something deeply suspect about those who think they know what is absolutely right on everything and feel entitled to judge everyone else accordingly.

My conclusion is that we are beginning to make progress in voicing our objections to pornography, whether it be changes in advertising or the different sort of behaviour at the motor-show. Even *The Sun* removed its pornographic picture from Page 3 to a later page in the paper for a few months. Journalists tell me that this was significant because Page 3 is a very important page – the first that confronts anyone who opens the paper. It is now, however, back in its old spot . . .

I also believe that the public debate on women's objection to pornography has liberated many women who now feel able to voice their feelings because they know that so many others agree with them. There has certainly been a change in the coverage of the issue in the quality press who no longer simply mock those who raise such objections. *The Times, The Guardian, The Daily Telegraph, The Financial Times* have all run serious articles – some support my view, others do not, but at least the issue is now being discussed.

But none of this means that all is well. I received a letter a few months ago from a woman who was dragged into a house and raped by a man who was watching ugly pornographic videos as he did it. I recently met a young woman graduate engineer who had left her profession because she felt that the men constantly used pornography to tell her that she was not welcome. Young men are still growing up learning about women from the porn they consume. Young women are constantly meeting the suggestion that this is the way that they should look and act if they wish to be considered a proper woman. Children are being sexually abused. Women are being raped.

If we think about it for too long, it can be deeply distressing. But this is not the only thing in life and for me it is only a part of my work. In so many ways women are growing and strengthening and demanding change. This is one part of it. We must be angry about the bad things but relish the good. We will build a better, kinder, more civilised world. The challenge to pornography is part of the journey.

While I was checking the proofs for *Dear Clare* . . . , the Home Office published the results of a review of existing research evidence on the effects of pornography.* Interestingly, the report was widely misrepresented in the media as claiming that there was no link between pornography and sexual violence. In fact the report says that it is not possible from the available research to decide whether or not pornography causes sexual violence. It also adds that claims that pornography is beneficial in creating outlets for men who might otherwise engage in sexual violence are also unproven. The report concedes that many women do find pornography distressing, and that women staying in hostels as a result of domestic violence frequently had partners who used pornography heavily. The report also admits that some sexual offenders used pornography heavily, – including in their prep-aration for their offence – but argues that this does not demonstrate that pornography was the *cause* of the offence. On pornography in the Press, the report states on page 90 that 'it might be that sexually violent pornography is the most dangerous but that newspaper nudity is still to a small degree harmful and because newspapers are more everyday than extreme porno-graphy their aggregate effects might be greater. The research evidence is silent on this.'

Despite these conclusions *The Sun* rang my researcher to ask whether as a result of the findings of the report I intended to call off my campaign against Page 3 pornography. I didn't bother to return the call: those who are determined to misrepresent even a Home Office report are unlikely to quote what I say fairly.

---

* 'Pornography: Impacts and Influences – A review of the available research evidence on the effects of pornography', Dennis Howitt and Guy Cumberbatch, commissioned by the Home Office Research and Planning Unit 1990.

A Woman's Place is in the House

Parliament and Power

The most striking thing about the letters was how broad-based support for Clare Short was. It was not simply a rallying round of Left wing or feminist supporters and was definite proof – if ever proof was needed – that on women's issues no one party has the monopoly and that no party adequately addresses our needs. In the debate following Clare Short's introduction of the Bill to ban Page 3, women had witnessed the failure of the democratic process. It was a revelation.

Women wrote in to express their solidarity with her for several reasons: to endorse her right to speak on behalf of them on this issue, given Robert Adley MP's assertion that she spoke only for herself; to say how directly porn had affected them; and to object in the strongest possible terms to the way she was treated in the House of Commons.

The debate focused for many women the inadequacies of our Parliamentary system. Parliament is organised in such a way that women's issues will always be subjugated to other priorities. In 1983, out of 276 women who stood for Parliament, only 23 were elected. In 1987 the figure had increased to 325, of which 41 were elected. In November 1990 as the new Prime Minister John Major announced his all-male cabinet, the number of women MPs was still less than 7% of the total.* This lack of proper political representation means that women must either exchange their individual voices and concerns for a group voice which will best serve their common interests as women, or risk these interests not being addressed at all. Women MPs are needed to represent women.

Hard won institutional changes are without value when society's basic perception of women remains unchanged. The right to vote, in practice, is often the right to vote for a man, and

* The Three Hundred Group, November 1990.

one who may fail to represent you properly in Parliament. Rights to equal pay are irrelevant if employers still consider men more able than women to do certain jobs and hire them in preference. Women want to act as individuals but are often prevented from achieving this status in the eyes of society through the persistence of men treating them as variations on a single sexual theme.

Sexual harassment is not just the groping of an occasional pervert but the systematic denial of rights that has become institutional to such an extent in this culture that when one woman stands up and puts an opposing view she is shouted down. This issue showed women that the sexism they suffered was in the very machinery of the State. Institutional harassment directly affects women's social progress. This was not a personal issue, it was a political one.

When Clare Short spoke to the House of Commons, she challenged masculine ideals on very masculine territory. Her woman's viewpoint was dismissed. MPs denied her experience because it challenged the validity of their own. It was a gender based power struggle writ large. Because men have laid the ground rules and arguments take place within them, men are rarely asked to qualify or justify their arguments. People may argue against them but they do not deny them the right to raise their questions. Women's experience is entirely different. They are continually asked to justify their reasons in making a point. Men aren't used to listening, women aren't used to speaking. It is easy to see how a political stalemate has developed.

This is unfortunate but inevitable. How can women operate comfortably in a structure that excludes them? How can men expect women to take part in an assembly which operates along the lines of an old boy's club; that starts at 2 pm and can remain open all night; that provides no creche facilities but still has room for a rifle range? Is it any wonder if women MPs sometimes behave like one of the boys, or in ways which they know will be acceptable to the boys, in order to fit in. Edwina Currie was cheered when she spoke of her wish to look like Samantha Fox, the better to please her husband.

In the absensce of an ideal world, Parliament exists to redress the balance. That is its job. In an ideal world we wouldn't need legislation, but since we do, this country's representative body has a duty to set precedents and impose guidelines while conducting itself in a manner that befits its responsibility. It is the job of MPs to take seriously any grievance which is laid before them.

Women were shocked at the insensitivity and foolishness of

MPs and their inability to debate seriously the matters Clare Short raised. Many wrote in from constituencies where their MP had voted against the Bill,* proving that in this instance Clare Short was better qualified to represent them than their own MPs. In a week where a rape in Ealing had been nationally reported and the usual outcry had been made about a violent society, here was an opportunity to discuss methods to address the problem. That opportunity was rejected out of hand by Parliament – and the tabloid press – because the solution it suggested was one of male accountability.

I AM A middle-aged, fulfilled woman with a lovely husband and two well adjusted normal daughters in their twenties and I agree with you completely (although a life long Conservative – but this really is above politics). Of course it doesn't disturb the normal man, who thinks it a bit of fun, but it's not those men we're talking about. I was absolutely disgusted at the way you were treated, and as for that Conservative lady (can't remember her name) who said she wished she looked like it – well just how stupid can you get. (Just remembered, it was Edwina Currie – well I won't think much of her in future.) I'm not a prude or jealous or anything in that vein, just feel that anything that can be done to try and stop all these horrific sex (and other) attacks on women should be done, and anything that might eliminate it – such as Page 3 girls – bought for a few pence, because I realise there are other mags even more explicit, but they cost a lot more. Sorry this is a bit of a jumble but just felt I had to write and give you my support.

TOWN WITHHELD

THE REACTION OF the Tory press and of the Tory boors, was sad and predictable, but it just provides a gauge of the hostility which women face when they attempt to analyse and challenge the way they are treated and portrayed in every sphere of life.

In the absence of less distorted and more realistic portrayals of

* See *Hansard* entries for 12 March 1986 (p *xix*) and 13 April 1988 (p *xxvii*).

women, illustrating the aspects of women's lives which do not conform to the popular press's stereotypes, it is hardly surprising that such hostile attitudes persist. So many women have unfortunately got themselves tied into knots through trying to define what might be 'acceptable' pornography, or what exactly constitutes offensive images of women, but it is surely not without reason that women often feel Page 3 of *The Sun* to be not in their own best interests and that it represents the thin end of the wedge.

In the end I suppose it all comes down to just who has the power in society to define our reality and our understanding of the world, as newspapers attempt to do, and as men in general are in a position to do in the world at large. Maybe, many years from now, people will look back on the reaction your bill received with the same kind of incredulity and disgust that we now look back on similar reactions to proposals that working people and women should have the vote – not that Page 3 will be banned, but that the way society views and treats women will be so alien and such an antithesis to that of present society, that it will simply have no reason to exist.

LINCOLNSHIRE

I FEEL THAT these representatives of the people have not begun to think through the basics of their attitudes. They obviously cannot separate their own sexuality (which is stimulated by female nudity) from the objective question of sexual mores in society. (While every male judge and juryman identifies with the rapist rather than the victim, how can we have justice?)

TOWN WITHHELD

I AM CONVINCED that these pictures of naked women with coy 'temptress' expressions only serve to confirm the current attitude that rape victims 'ask for it'. It frightens me that intelligent human beings in Parliament should oppose your Bill, even more that they should ridicule it.

HAMPSHIRE

IN THE KIND of male dominated society in which we live, it will take ages for men to realise that they cannot tell us what we find offensive . . . It is time that MPs realised the kind of moral decay they are actively encouraging throughout our society by allowing national papers to carry this kind of porn.

OXFORD

PEOPLE WHO ASK why women do not put themselves forward for a political life need look no further than today's *The Guardian** for an explanation. You must be a brave and determined woman to put forward your Bill. I flinched in sympathy at the response you got. Some of your colleagues should be careful when they express their contempt for women – some of us are listening and some of us will not forget what we have heard.

EAST YORKSHIRE

AS FOR THE Mr Adleys – I know revenge is rarely commendable, but such things often have a way of evening out in the long run. Perhaps when women are eventually represented more appropriately in Parliament by an appropriately large number of women, I hope we find the Mr Adleys have been replaced by women. He, at least, would then have more time to pursue the 'few pleasures left' to him – by then, let's hope they have been further reduced by one. Poor man.

FIFE

I WAS FURIOUS to hear the guffaws and sexist remarks from some of your fellow MPs when I listened to Parliament on the radio, reporting the debate of your Bill. As a woman, and knowing that there are only 25 women MPs in Parliament, I feel totally alienated by that institution.

TOWN WITHHELD

* Andrew Rawnsley's 'Parliamentary Diary', *The Guardian*, 14 April 1988.

HOW, I WONDER, would most men feel if it was their mother, wife or daughter exposing their bodies for other men to ogle? Would it still be 'harmless fun'? Yet it is alright for them to ogle someone else's daughter . . . What hypocrisy.

BEDFORDSHIRE

EVIDENTLY THE THREAT to the male ego regarding competition is so great that male Page 3s are outlawed – women may start comparing them and even forget to look at their bowler hats.

TOWN WITHHELD

MANY WOMEN, I am sure, cannot voice their support for your endeavours for fear of being regarded as prudes. This is a label that we will just have to live with I'm afraid.

TOWN WITHHELD

I AM PROUD that so many other women of whatever political persuasion are standing by you. It is time women's issues crossed the political divide so that we can all unite against the real opposition – tired, sick old men who throw this filth at us and then shed crocodile tears when another woman or child is dragged out of the river.

TOWN WITHHELD

I HAVE BROUGHT up three sons, the youngest is now 18 and I am sure they could look at these pictures without any lasting effects because they have been brought up in a loving and caring home. What we must realise is that there are large numbers of children who live in appalling conditions with indifferent or even cruel parents, and these pictures together with the violence and soft pornography with is part of the daily programme of the media, brutalise what little sensibility they have left. Perhaps those Members of the House who sniggered when the Bill was raised would not be so amused if a youth whose mind had been twisted in such a way, were to assault or rape a member of their own family. Then they would raise their hands in pious horror as they have done at the recent events at the vicarage at Ealing.*

TOWN WITHHELD

I AM BURSTING to write to you for the following reasons:

To stand up and be counted with you.

To declare my position in case I'm in danger of being lumped with 'the vast majority'† of women who do not, supposedly, object to such material.

To agree with you that I am deeply concerned about the connection between photographs or 'literature' – which we are told is harmless – and deepseated attitudes towards sex and sexuality in our society which degrade both men and women.

To express my disbelief at the crude and immature attitudes and behaviour of people representing us in Parliament towards this matter.

Also to express my disgust that this matter be so frivolously dealt with by the 'Honourable Gentlemen' at a time when our morning news tells us a doctor has raped an 8-year-old girl, and a programme last night on our TV screens tells us that 1 in 6 women in Britain have been raped, and 1 in 4 in the US.

CHESHIRE

I WAS DISGUSTED to read about the childish reception given to your Indecent Displays Bill by supposedly intelligent Members of the House. It is difficult enough to convince my liberal-minded male student friends of the dangers of breakfast table pornography, let alone the jaded old men in the Tory party (inspired no

* This rape, in March 1986, was given a great deal of detailed coverage by the tabloid press. *The Sun*, controversially, published a photograph of the rape 'survivor' on its front page. In the same week, *The Daily Mirror* ran a feature called 'Bloody Brutal Britain' (14 March 1986) which catalogued the high incidence of recent sexual assaults. No editorial considered the possibility of links between sexual violence and pornography.

† In opposing the Bill, Robert Adley MP said 'to suggest seriously . . . that these pictures are offensive to the overwhelming majority of women is inaccurate' (see p. xxvii).

doubt by Edwina Currie's ridiculous comments) and the macho 'socialists' who ought to know better.

WHY DO WE always have to wait for proof, which is usually impossible to get anyway, when one's instincts suggest that the self-indulgent media are encouraging a constantly lowering moral tone, which has a good chance of raising sex crime levels . . . However, while we have MPs such as Martin Brown and our own Nicholas Baker (in my experience he talks to the men and thanks the women for the refreshments) there is little hope for women to be at last treated with respect.

DORSET

WHAT A LONELY battle you have against the nauseating behaviour of your Right wing colleagues in the House. Just hearing those men baying and jeering out their prejudices made my blood run cold.

Do people who expound their theories of 'Pornography for All' ever stop to think of the consequences for those people actually involved – let alone those who buy the stuff? As long as there is poverty and ignorance women will sell what they have and men will exploit it. Just thinking about the misery of child prostitution makes me sick. And saying that Page 3 has nothing to do with society's attitude to women defies belief.

Yes, I am a feminist although I am married with four children – and two stepchildren – so I'm not a prude (how I hate having to defend my stand) but someone, somewhere must make a stand for our children's future and I'm proud to know it's another woman.

BRIGHTON

THE WORST THING about all this is that until the subject is 'politicised' as you are doing, it cannot be discussed without one being put down as overeducated, snobbish or plain frigid.

I AM A 30-year-old married woman – fairly liberal minded, I'd like to think – but I fear you have a long hard battle ahead of you. I can only wonder that if the House was full of women instead of men (who mostly approve of these pictures, let's face it) that your passage would be much quicker, and more fully understood.

TOWN WITHHELD

OVER THE YEARS I have spent many hours arguing with my husband and with male colleagues about why it is that women find Page 3 girls demeaning and degrading to our sex. Many men simply cannot understand what it is to be treated as an object and if they themselves have no violent tendencies, they cannot make the link between these provocative models invading the nation's breakfast tables, and sexual violence.

TOWN WITHHELD

HOW WOULD MR Adley feel, I wonder, were the tables turned, and he was sitting on the tube confronted by a group of sniggering girls ogling a Page 3 male model, discussing the size and shape of his 'Page 3' and then staring directly at certain parts of Mr Adley's anatomy as if in comparison. I guess that he would not enjoy his tube journeys in quite the same comfort as he states he does at present.

TOWN WITHHELD

IT SEEMS THAT one member of the Tory party thinks it is more important that he is kept amused whilst sitting on underground trains watching the faces of people pretending not to be reading Page 3 rather than trying to do all in his power to change the dangerous attitudes of a minority of men in this country towards the opposite sex.

TOWN WITHHELD

I BELIEVE THAT it is disgusting and degrading that women should be subjected to rude comments from men who think this kind of thing is funny. I am a 13-year-old girl and know I speak for my class at school when I say it is about time something should be done. How are we to make our point clear if the only answers we get are 'Oh you're jealous' or 'it is one of the few pleasures left in life'. I would be grateful if you could let the MPs who oppose you know that if *The Sun*'s Page 3 is one of the few pleasures in life, his life cannot be worth much, and I dread to think what sort of MP he must be.

TOWN WITHHELD

IT'S A PITY Robert Adley wasn't on the underground watching people's faces yesterday instead of sitting in Parliament making facile comments.

TOWN WITHHELD

I'VE WANTED TO throw a brick through the newsagent's window for so long – *please* throw one through Mr Adley's smug facade for me. You have my heartfelt support but is there anything useful I can do?

LANCASHIRE

I WAS MOST taken aback to hear elected representatives, all men of course, deriding the opinions of a substantial number of women. One chap seemed more interested in watching '*The Sun* readers' than in seriously questioning the effect such visual stimuli might have on men's attitudes to women and women's feelings about their own place in society.

If apparently intelligent men take this view what hope is there for the man on the Clapham Omnibus?

TOWN WITHHELD

EVEN IF IT doesn't get through at least the issue has been aired; some people have been provoked to think a bit about our 'tit' orientated culture. As for the response to your motion by that wally of an MP Robert Adley, I find it a bit frightening that an adult holding a responsible job in Government can trivialise a serious issue that deals with sexual crimes and the degradation of women to such an extent . . . I'm surprised you managed to get the Bill that far in the male-dominated House of Commons.

TOWN WITHHELD

ARE THESE MEN really appointed by public vote?

LANCASHIRE

THEY KNOW 52% of the people they are supposed to represent find these pictures offensive. They know many young boys have this way of viewing women and their sexuality thrust upon them – doing untold damage to a weak impressionable mind and maybe leading to sexual crimes – they just don't give a damn.

Fortunately, they have no logical counters to your argument for the Bill. All they can do is behave as though they were at a pantomime booing the wicked witch.

LONDON

NEEDLESS TO SAY I am shocked, though not surprised, by the reaction of male MPs – I had expected such predictable speeches from the Tory ranks but I am even more disgusted (if that is possible) by the behaviour of Austin Mitchell or Andrew Faulds in voting against the Bill. I wonder when these men have had to live with the consequences of frequent sexual attack or abuse? It is clear they have no conception of what it is like to live with the constant threat of such crimes, as I and other millions of women do. To us such daily displays in the newspapers of female nudity or semi-nudity portrayed in such a degrading manner, appears to condone the the actual sexual degradation which many of us have suffered and will continue to suffer.

TOWN WITHHELD

AFTER READING ALL the pig-ignorant remarks made by sexist half-wits about your Bill, I felt I had to write . . . It amazes me when I see MPs griping about law and order and life sentences for rapists and failing completely to grasp the idea that rape is caused by the way women are portrayed in society, as whores, as available, as there for the taking. Why can't people see that rape is to a large extent preventable?

Don't let the idiots get to you.

MANCHESTER

I AM SURE that there are many women like myself whose blood boiled at the reaction you received in the House of Commons to the subject of soft porn in newspapers. I was surprised at this irresponsible attitude, and wonder how so many people with power and authority in the country, and access to the facts and figures, could refuse to see the facts clearly presented to them. Surely anything which distorts men's attitudes to women and sex, and can influence children and impressionable adolescents, should be banned from a society which sees itself as civilised?

TOWN WITHHELD

I FEEL THAT I must write and convey my disgust at the baying and howling of your male colleagues in response to your speech.

The news for the past few days has been filled with the tragic reports of the rape of a vicar's daughter and of the disgraceful hounding she has suffered at the hands of the press. It seems incredible to me that the arrogant, patronising male MPs of this morning's broadcast can see no link between the way tabloids treat women in both of these situations.

Twelve years ago I was a victim of rape, and it is a bitterness against the press and some male authority figures that stays with me. The reaction of some MPs to your Bill was a sharp reminder to me of some of the comments made at the time my case came to trial.

TOWN WITHHELD

I WAS NOT surprised at some of the derogatory comments on your Bill by Mr Robert Adley, who obviously knows how to get a cheap laugh from his colleagues – or gang. If he were to debate the subject with you without an audience he would find that wisecracks are no substitute for an argument.

TOWN WITHHELD

I'M NEITHER NARROW minded, nor against men, or nudity come to that – we like to sunbathe in France on nudist beaches and are quite happy. It is the *intention* behind the photograph to denigrate women that I like intensely, and I was disgusted at the attitude of many men in the Chamber who have the same bullying tactic when women speak in the House.

TOWN WITHHELD

TO HEAR OUR so-called leaders and representatives behaving in this way shocked me to tears.

TOWN WITHHELD

I HOPE THAT I will be able to write a reasonably coherent letter. I have been quite literally shaking with anger on hearing about your abominable treatment by a section of your male colleagues last week, when you sought leave to introduce your Private Member's Bill. I despair when I think that these guffawing idiots – who would be more at home dressed in short pants with school caps on their addled heads, sitting in the fourth form and no doubt looking forward to playtime when they will congregate at the back of the cycle sheds with their copies of *The Sun* to snigger and drool over Page 3's outstanding assets. People actually vote for these specimens – I can't believe it . . .

CHESHIRE

AFTER LISTENING TO 'Yesterday in Parliament' earlier in the week, I was horrified at the onslaught that followed your talk on Page 3 daily newspaper features. I could not believe that I was listening to the business in the Houses of Parliament, a rugby football club at 11 pm on a Saturday night – Yes – but a place where our elected members discuss the country's business – No. I was so horrified and appalled at the crude behaviour of the Tory backbenchers that joined in the haranguing that I have written to the Speaker of the House expressing my views. We do not stand together politically but I consider that irrelevant. No one should have to take the kind of vulgar attack that you were subjected to. I wish you every success with your motion and will follow with interest any changes of attitude that it may bring about. I do believe that if you expose the human form to ridicule and cheap thrills, in the process you lower respect and the degree of sensitivity is lowered to the point where violation becomes easier. I think that history has shown that when you have lowered something to ridicule and contempt the next step is wanting power over it. I see rape not so much as a sexual thing but a desire for power with violence/fear.

LEICESTER

HOW DARE THE *Sun* and other garbage newspapers scream so indignantly about the horrors of rape and violence when a turn of its front page produces the very imagery that, to my mind, could spark off the feelings about and towards women – all women – that produce these attacks. Nor let us forget that though not all women may be raped and beaten physically, we are still viewed with a mixture of lust and loathing by many men, as was implied in Mr Adley's reported comment 'Your speech was a titillating mixture of politics, prejudice and prurience. It is barely credible . . .'. Pat on the head. We've humoured you enough. It's only sour grapes because you'd never get on to Page 3. Only ugly lesbians don't like the pictures etc, etc.

Wrong, Mr Adley, or should we say Addledly? There are plenty of us who are neither ugly nor lesbian nor jealous – though if we were ugly or lesbian would we not still have the right to an opinion? We just want this ugly practice stopped.

KENT

WE FEEL THAT the continual portrayal of women as objects of male sexual fantasy, rather than as individual human beings, is a way of maintaining and colluding with traditional notions of women as being powerless. As sexual abuse of women is the brutal manifestation of male power, we feel very strongly that male images and definitions of women must be challenged and redefined.

One very clear example of the way men humiliate women was seen in the response you received from many male MPs when you raised the issue in the House . . .

GLOUCESTERSHIRE

THAT SOME MEMBERS of the Commons should have received this with levity shows how necessary it was for you to draw attention to this pernicious way of presenting an image of women in a way which panders to undesirable male attitudes.

CHESHIRE

Tit for Tat

The Gutter Press Exposed

Women rallied to support the premise of Clare Short's Bill opposing the widespread acceptance of pornographic images of women in national newspapers. They felt that Page 3 *was* pornography; that it institutionalises the sexual subordination of women to a mass market, cheaply and on a daily basis, and should therefore be relegated to pornographic magazines.

Newspapers are our touchstone for the world. They hold a relatively sacred place in our society and we rely on them to inform us on world and national events. The presence of Page 3 in daily newspapers gives pornography a status it does not deserve. It makes a fantasy notion of women available where all else is purported to be fact. Many women do not feel that Page 3 is a factual or even fair representation of women but its presence encourages men to see all women in the light of it. Men are discouraged from using their analytic capabilities to sift out the fact from the fiction.

The physical attractiveness and willingness to please is the primary newsworthiness of *all* women in the papers as exemplified by the bare-breasted Page 3 girl. No matter who she is or what she has done, her hair colour and age are always more important. Ordinary stories are given lewd angles to give them a sexy flavour. In the tabloids, rape stories are newsworthy only in so far as they can be dramatised and sensationalised and add a textual dimension to the pages where the naked women appear.* Throughout, these papers judge, mock and dismiss women revealing the hypocrisy of their 'family' stance.

Of *The Sun*'s majority of male readers almost half are under 35

---

* However, no newspaper has a completely clean record so far as the reporting of rape is concerned. Rape stories are often put in at the trial stage, where details make salacious reading, but the verdict is less frequently given space. The press also disproportionately reports rape by a stranger, whereas the majority of attacks are actually by men known to the woman (see *The Independent*, 14 November 1990).

(and a significant number under the age of 24).* Given this market, tabloid attitudes – far from pandering to an existing desire, actually create it by telling the impressionable, curious and inexperienced what is attractive and what they should find sexy. Moreover, it encourages readers to believe that women are not likely to offer any resistance or objections to being judged in this way or being judged at all. That Page 3 has become a national and daily institution has led men to expect and anticipate its appearance. It has become the right of the popular press buying public to have 'tits' as soon as they turn the page. The dangerous situation of *expecting* the availability of a woman's body cannot always be contained as a fantasy notion within the pages of a newspaper.†

If this is what sells newspapers, then we ought to look at the price of the sale. The women who pose for Page 3 were regarded by many of the women who wrote in as blameless because their occupation is one of the few opportunities for women in this society to earn large sums of money. But the wages they earn and the status they can achieve must be put into some social context. The Page 3 woman earns her salary by selling the rights of all women to their individual privacy. Futhermore, she makes money from parodying and playing up to male fantasies of, say, schoolgirl or nurse, making the real life positions of these women very difficult. Fantasy nurses get paid more than real ones. The huge wages paid to individual models is still a poor wage for oppression and it is a price paid daily, not by the newspaper barons, but by women everywhere.

Page 3 pictures were introduced in *The Sun* on 17 November 1970. By 1972 circulation had nearly doubled.‡ The naked bodies of pubescent women have been hijacked to sell newspapers by the men who own them. The sales ploy and the product have become so confused that the disposability of that product and of the women that sold it to you have become one and the same thing. This commercial abuse presents women as a disposable commodity to be used up and thrown away. This fact cannot be separated from the violent abuse of women in society and the rise in rape and assault figures.

Graphic rape reports are designed, say the tabloids, 'to shock us out of complacency which increasingly allows women and

* News International Advertising Services Department, November 1990.
† On 27 April 1986 *The News of the World* invited readers to 'Spot a Page 3 Girl with her Clothes On!' at various seaside resorts. If they apprehended the right women, they were promised a 'crisp tenner and a kiss'.
‡ Benn's Newspaper Press Directory

children to fall prey to horrific attacks . . . we have a duty to protect them.'* Many women comment in their letters on the hypocrisy and double standards of tabloid journalism where salacious reporting and moral editorials are often at odds with each other. They also comment on the absence of naked men and jokingly suggest ways in which this imbalance might be corrected.

I AM WRITING to express my support for your campaign to ban topless pin-up girls in daily newspapers, which I believe – and hope – you still pursue in spite of the vilification you have received as a result of it. It is perfectly obvious to me that to present women explicitly as sex objects, to be viewed in such inappropriate settings as at the breakfast table, or on the bus to work in the morning, cannot fail to promote the view that women – *all* women – are purely sex objects. This is bound to make it difficult for men to relate to women as thinking human beings in non-sexual situations – let alone equals! One never sees Samantha Fox ogling a man, she is there to be chosen, not to choose! – and is also likely to encourage some men to feel that, since sex is what women are for, why shouldn't they take what they want, when and where they want it? And hence – sex crime.

It is also my belief that some of this rubs off on women – some women view themselves as sex objects – with the result that they live half-lives, living and acting only to please men & become obsessively concerned with their own appearance, believing they have to live up to some sort of weird 'ideal'. The type of sexuality portrayed by Page 3 is passive, silent, hardly consistent with fulfilling a useful, complete life to one's full potential outside the bedroom.

But why is the reaction so hysterical from Page 3 lovers? I believe that men who like these pictures (not those who glance at them in passing because they're there, but those who *really* like them, buy papers specially, put the pictures on the wall, look at them for hours) do so because they are sexually deprived. They are, or believe themselves to be, physically or socially inadequate and cannot form the fulfilling and satisfying relationships with

*The News of the World, 16 March 1986.

flesh and blood women, so they have fantasy relationships with Page 3 girls – who are always ready and willing, never say no, never complain at the physical performance or make demands, whose eyes cannot see the puny arms or the beer belly, who don't have to be impressed with witty conversation, who don't have a voice or a choice, who are not a threat. These are the men whom men are led to believe they ought to be like and whom women are led to believe they ought to satisfy! This is pitiable, pathetic, but, taken to extremes, in some cases this sex-without-relationships complex could lead to sex crimes.

Congratulations, Clare, for having the guts to stand up and say what I did not have the courage to stand up and say. It's a hard battle – years of societal conditioning have got us to where we are now, when a girl is called 'darling' and looked up and down, regardless of the situation and how likely it is to lead to sex and however irrelevant her appearance might be. Perhaps women ought to start staring at the groin of every man she meets – I think the Page 3 fans would not enjoy such close scrutiny!

I know it must be hard when people write to newspapers making intelligent remarks like 'Clare Short looks bad enough with her clothes on, let alone off', – one wonders what the author of that remark looks like without his clothes on!! But such tripe merely demonstrates the petty-minded stupidity of the writer – and also how much he sees you, a woman with 'muscle' and a voice, who will not be put down by moronic insults, as a threat! Women have for centuries been put down by personal insults – the same men who love Page 3 fantasy also seem to believe that the worst thing you can say to a woman is to question her attractiveness, and for years women – like me – have allowed this to get to us and have shut up to avoid it. You represent the opposite to the Page 3 view of women – you are definitely not a passive toy, you definitely are a thinking, speaking human being – and therefore a threat to poor little men! Wouldn't it be awful if all women were that way!!

Don't be knocked down by the sewer-mouthed, sewer-brained morons who are afraid of their own penises. Know that you are right, know that women *and* men in droves support and admire you, know that only the stupid and/or mentally screwed-up could really disagree, and continue to say what silly creatures like me are too scared and intimidated to say & continue to set an example to us all. I would rather my daughters had you as a role model than Samantha Fox!

BIRMINGHAM

I HAVE ALWAYS thought that the silly ideas of female passivity and sexuality preached by *The Sun* and *The Star* do more harm than real pornography, but I am sure basically decent boys are misled by newspaper images. God knows men are hard enough to convince that female sexuality isn't just a coy and teasing version of male lust as it is.

TOWN WITHHELD

I AM QUITE horrified to think that if I was to have a young son under the age of 18 he would be quite able to go into the nearest newsagent and purchase a copy of *The Sun*, or similar publications, and see a picture of a semi-naked woman, whereas if he was to attempt to purchase a copy of *Penthouse* for example he would almost certainly be refused because of the content of the magazine. This seems ludicrous when after all the pictures in *The Sun* do not exactly leave much to the imagination and yet the law says this sort of thing is acceptable. Quite typical, I think, of the fact that the majority of people making laws are men.

GLOUCESTER

I HATE ALL pornography, because it reduces people to lumps of meat. Also it sets up hierarchies which make people's lives unhappy: you're not a real woman unless you look like those 'pretty girls'. *The Sun* is different to porno mags because it gets used as newspaper for household and other purposes, which then makes pornography part of our everyday lives, and children, who are impressionable, get used to seeing women in that role: rubber doll.

TOWN WITHHELD

ALTHOUGH I AM not a reader of *The Sun* I have been buying it this week to read what they have to say about the Page 3 issue. In today's paper I see they are calling Selina Scott and yourself 'killjoys' because of your attitudes.* I would like to offer you some support as

* *The Sun*, 10 April 1986.

I have been called this in my own house by my own husband because of my own strong feelings on the subject. My husband wouldn't bother to buy a girlie mag but thinks as most men do, because these pics are in a paper it's all right to look at them. Our menfolk wouldn't like it one bit if we were 'oohing and aahing' over pictures of beautiful young males with very well endowed sexual attributes. Not that I would advocate publishing these pictures in daily papers (although a picture of a naked man would at least provide a balance) – as it is, these papers are still intent on perpetuating the idea in men's heads that it is their right to look at other women's nakedness and to see women as sex objects.

N. IRELAND

I HAVE THREE small children, three cats, innumerable stick insects and am in the throes of moving house, but I cannot let another day go by without thanking you and congratulating you on tackling an issue that is crucially important to every person in the country. I loathe and abhor the Page 3 mentality that allows semi-naked women to be leered at over the breakfast table and folded over fish and chips for supper. It upsets me in a way that surprises even myself and I feel so comforted that at least someone is actually confronting society with its own degradation. For Page 3 degrades women but it also degrades men who leer. I have nothing against the models – who in these hard up times can blame them for making money out of men's fatuousness? – although it is sad that basically good-natured girls should collaborate in the diminution of their own sex. Neither do I object to their nakedness. I love the classic paintings and their exultation of the beauty of the female body. I don't even wish to end the soft pornography that can titillate harmlessly the inadequate men who like that sort of thing. What I find utterly humiliating and infuriating is the acceptability of sexual in-equality which daily pin-ups in a newspaper seeks to preserve. The implicit message of 'just a bit of fun' is that males may continue to refuse to take women seriously.

OXFORD

I PERSONALLY FEEL very embarrassed reading or watching someone read a newspaper with a Page 3 or Page 7 girl showing. Also I find the strong editorials of *The Sun* 'slamming' rape and assaults against women to be pure hypocrisy, as they are encouraging people to view women's bodies as objects to be gloated over, as part of general news items. Photos of topless women should only be allowed in the 'adult' magazines which are not open for children's viewing. The worst part is the accessibility of these newspapers to everyone, so children grow up accepting these 'panting beauties' to be normal. Topless models have no place in a family newspaper.

EASTBOURNE

I WRITE IN support of your Bill. My only regret is that its provisions would not apply to text as well as pictures. I was genuinely horrified to see that *The Sun*, on the same day that it reported the vicarage rape (and photographed the victim) carried a centre page feature devoted to the 'fact' that most women fantasise about being 'stripped and made love to by an entire football team'.*

LONDON

IF THE GOVERNMENT in passing legislation to make seat belts compulsory infringed on civil liberties in order to save lives as pressure failed, then surely stories of sex and rape in newspapers should not be elaborated on in the salacious way they are and also newspapers should be forbidden to publish provocative female photographs with sexual intention . . . If that ban could save one woman from being raped, it is good enough to become law.

TOWN WITHHELD

WHAT REALLY MADE my blood boil, and probably incited me to write this letter was *The Sun* . . . I was flicking through a copy discarded on the train yesterday, and was absolutely disgusted to see a front page picture of the vicar's daughter who was raped. If that wasn't enough, in a piece of drivel in the middle pages

* *The Sun*, 10 April 1986.

entitled 'Women's Fantasies' (ha) apparently the number three fantasy of us women is being taken by force. Well, my blood was boiling. (I know what my favourite fantasy is now and it involves the Editor of *The Sun* and a pair of pliers.) All I can say is it's no wonder men seem to think all women who are raped enjoy it really and are all asking for it. How can it be that a newspaper is allowed to print this rubbish? As a victim of a sexual attack myself, the attacker later saying in court that he was provoked by pornography, maybe I feel more strongly about this than most.

BUCKINGHAMSHIRE

FOR A LONG time I've felt there's something very contradictory about the 'popular' daily newspapers which report rapes in tones of horror and then print pictures which demean and insult women. Only a couple of weeks ago there was a classic case of crass hypocrisy in *The Daily Mirror* – on the front page there was a lot of self-congratulation about *The Daily Mirror*'s exposure of certain pornographic services being offered via British Telecom, then on Page 3 we were presented with exactly the same kind of demeaning image of women they'd just condemned.★ Of the two, I think the visual images are by far the most insidious, not simply for what they are – there is much worse material available elsewhere after all – but for the context. Having such images as a fixed feature in papers that are read by and aimed at not only men but also women and children, makes this portrayal of women into an everyday 'normal' and acceptable thing. I've heard this 'Oh its everywhere, you've only got to open the morning paper' attitude used by men as an argument for putting up pornographic calendars in workplaces. And then where do you draw the line? We must not be afraid of being thought prudes when we feel something is offensive and damaging to us as women. It's easy for us to turn over Page 3 quickly to avoid embarassment, but only by saying loud and clear that we *won't accept* them will such things be made unacceptable.

My friends and I think you're very courageous to do this publicly, and we wish you well in your campaign.

LEEDS

★ *The Daily Mirror*, February 1986.

I CONSIDER SUCH photographs to be objectionable on feminist grounds, a potentially harmful influence on the young, and utterly irrelevant in newspapers.

TOWN WITHHELD

WE'RE BRANDED 'PRUDES' I know, but at least our minds are free of pollution from the gutter press pictures.

TOWN WITHHELD

AS YOU RIGHTLY say, if men wish to look at pictures of naked women there are plenty of magazines which cater for their tastes. All the women we know find it embarrassing, crude and totally irrelevant to see them in ordinary newspapers.

LONDON

MANY WOMEN NOW realise that the obscenity problem is much closer to home, widely available and freshly published every morning on Page 3. The continuity is disturbing: whether the page in question is used for a cat litter tray or is defaced by a felt tip pen, next morning a brand new 'lovely' appears. In an era of *disposable* consumer goods, are we fostering such attitudes towards women?

TOWN WITHHELD

IT STRIKES ME as ridiculous in this so-called 'equal' age that daily newspapers which are written and produced for the benefit of *all* citizens particularly wage earners are still aimed at and geared up for men – male sports pages (football, darts etc) and advertising using female bodies to sell anything from teabags to car oil. Without a doubt the Page 3 girls are the most offensive indicating quite clearly that women are to be regarded as objects, toys or an accessory to the male sports car.

If women are to be treated as equals, they must be treated as such by the media; ie you do not see 'attractive male 24 . . .' or 'half naked' or 'poor attractive divorced male attacked by ex-wife'. Your Page 3 Bill will be the first step up the ladder and not before time – after all fair play, decency and equality should be something all politicians can rise to.

TOWN WITHHELD

WHAT I TAKE exception to (I take *The Daily Mirror* daily) is the assumption of many newspaper editors that only men read their papers. For example, phrases like 'choose your Page 3 girl of the year, *folks*'.

ESSEX

RESPECT FOR WOMEN emanates in the home; and I feel very sorry for the children whose parents have brought them up to respect women, and to value real love, only to find that women are regarded by men who buy papers like *The Sun* primarily in terms of physical sexual gratification – an image made particularly unpleasant by the fact that the Page 3 girls often have baby-like, vacuous faces, encouraging male notions of aggression and possession. If a stop could be put on the publication of this type of press exploitation – which, unlike porn books, is seen by millions of children and adolescents – it would be an excellent practical step towards encouraging respect towards women as *people*. Of what use is the 'liberation' of women, when such hypocritical exploitation is being allowed in the mass circulation press, which gobbles up its greedy profits mainly because of this exploitation?

LONDON

I AM WRITING in support of your attempts to rid the daily papers of the 'boobs and bottoms' syndrome. Given the influence of the 'press barons' and the vastly disproportionate number of men to women in Parliament, I fear your efforts will meet with failure.

TOWN WITHHELD

I HOPE YOUR Bill is the first step of many needed to protect the women and children of this country against the perversions exacerbated by some people who will cater to any tastes in order to increase their profits.

GALLOWAY

I HAVE PREVIOUSLY written to Mrs Thatcher suggesting a standard of decency should be maintained by newspapers (which at present often resemble porn magazines) but I fear the Tory Government will always put the interests of businessmen like Rupert Murdoch before the safety of ordinary women . . .

I have tried to see the other side of the argument: ie would men take exception to a Page 3 man in highly revealing briefs as part of their morning reading? I think they would be highly irritated and despise women for demanding this sort of thing, and view it as a 'silly weakness'.

TOWN WITHHELD

A SUGGESTION RE your campaign on Page 3 nudes: how would your male colleagues react to male models nude from the waist downwards, with measurements of buttocks, balls, penis erect and flaccid? How would they cope with questions from their 10-year-old daughter?

Good luck, from one who is not a prude.

TOWN WITHHELD

DEAR MISS SHORT

Aren't you just the old spoilsport for spoiling the 'harmless' fun of *The Sun* readers.

It appears that if enough people want something it becomes harmless. Well, why stop at naked women? Let's have something for everyone; the possibilities are endless . . . Personally there is nothing I like better at breakfast than a coy picture of homo erectus on Page 3 of my *The Daily Telegraph*. Sets me up for the day. After that I might even be persuaded to swap my packet of soap powder for two of Jimmy Young's. Maybe I could persuade Eddie Shah to do a pop-up version.

OXFORDSHIRE

IN ORDER TO explain the outrageousness of what is being done to us, I wonder if it would be worthwhile producing a mock-up of *The Sun* with roles reversed, the same kind of rubbish written about women, and to describe all men in terms of their relationships with women, so that rather than reading 'vicar's daughter' one reads 'father of warehouse packer Irene Jones'. I honestly do not believe that most people are even aware of the constant denying of women in their own right, women with their own identities. It's so deeply ingrained in our society.

I have a career, a husband and a child and for the sake of all of them, and for the sake of this country, with its outdated, patriarchal society, I wish you one hundred percent success.

TOWN WITHHELD

THIS MORNING I went to a local newsagent to buy a newspaper. In *The Sunday Mirror* my attention was drawn to the 'girly' photograph taking up about one third of the front page. Sod it, I thought, I'm not paying 28 pence to be insulted – it would be as daft for example, as a black person buying a paper with a large insulting photograph of another black person on the front page. I am a working class woman, with a son of 20 who I've brought up to notice and question sexism, and he's turned out well balanced, has good relationships with women and I'm glad. But I wish something could be done on a huge scale.

I've been thinking hard about this problem. I think the way women are treated by the media – constantly presented numerous times a day as silly, frivolous, sexual objects and playthings for men – is a gross violation of human rights. Half the population is expected to ignore or accept stereotyped images of themselves; images which imply a lack of seriousness, a purpose in life mainly to give men pleasure, and images which imply that the most important components of a woman are her breasts and buttocks.

Under the circumstances it is the height of hypocrisy for the popular tabloids to express horror and shock when women are so often used for sexual relief then discarded or killed.

Possibly you think I'm exaggerating, calling this treatment of women an abuse of human rights, although I'm sure you understand very well what I mean. It is fairly simple to test if human rights are being violated if we take a hypothetical situation. If we turn the table around to give an analogy of what it would be like for men if they were used as sexual objects – and many good cartoons have been produced by women making this point – the situation every day would be something like this:

1.   Every single day of the week at least three national newspapers would have very large photographs of men – slim men, young men, beefy men, boyish men – posing, smiling (or in some cases pouting), wearing only the tiniest of G-strings around their bottoms and genitals, with silly copy attached to the photographs making them look even more foolish.

2.   Women in the newspapers would always be treated seriously, apart from a harmless little joke here and there, and would be described as for example, Brenda Jones, sales manager or Joan Smith, unwaged. Men on the other hand, would be described as handsome Howard Thomas, blond Richard Tate, or reported in some way designed to cause interest in their looks as opposed to their character or purpose in life.

3.   Television adverts would show good-looking, young men sliding their hands suggestively over their hips in their new briefs, saying how they like to look their best for women. Men in shampoo commercials will ballet dance saying how lovely and shiny their hair is and how happy it makes them.

4.   On television every night the theme of men being seduced, insulted, frightened, raped and murdered would run throughout many of the films and regular series seen. Often the men in the films would wear tight trousers and high cuban heels as they fled for their lives. Lots of other times they would be naked, having a shower, as the murderess creeps up on them.

5.   Every newsagent would have a shelf full of 'boys-mags', their glossy front page showing men, nude of course, holding their balls or bending over doing the splits or something. Feminists would be encouraged to buy these magazines to show to their friends and have a laugh over them, comparing the photographs and so on.

Wouldn't *all* the men just love it all?

I think that if these situations, and more, were really happening in the media today there would be massive protest from men. If their protests were brushed to one side – as our protests are currently – it would surely be a violation of human rights?

The taking of the case for women's human rights to court is something that I would dearly love to see happen. Previously, apart from Bills through Parliament (and I admire you tremendously over your recent attempt) and the possibility of persuading women to boycott sexist papers – I could see no other way forward.

LONDON

THE RECENT SENSATIONAL treatment of rapes and sex attacks, and the harassment by the press of a rape victim has shown the double standards that exist. I was appalled to learn from my husband, whose parents get *The News of the World*, that last Sunday in that paper there was an 'artist's reconstruction' of the attack on the vicar's daughter, which my husband said made the woman look as if she was in a provocative pose.*

TOWN WITHHELD

I CONSIDER THE editors of these papers to be a bunch of hypocrites, since any newspaper which openly condemns rape on its front cover and then has the audacity to display a provocative picture of a woman on the following page is completely out of order.

TOWN WITHHELD

IT INCENSES ME that a tabloid will carry a shock-horror rape story on one page, and then show their Page 3 girl on the next page, without acknowledging that the image of women as objects to be lusted over is the image which a rapist must have at the back of his mind.

TOWN WITHHELD

* *The News of the World*, 9 March 1986. The caption to this read 'An artist's impression of the horror scene as Spiderman drags the screaming girl towards the bedroom while his thug accomplice batters her father and boyfriend senseless with the vicar's own bat.' (The rapist had a tatoo of a spider's web on his arm.)

IT REALLY ANNOYS me when these so-called 'newspapers' pretend to take a moral tone and often print the story on the same page as the nudes.

LONDON

I READ WITH interest about your campaign to have 'pin-up' pictures banned from newspapers, and I am writing to put on record my *support* for your efforts.

I find these pictures *offensive*, (always have done from the days years ago when they were first included in the daily newspapers). Moreover, I do not see why people like me should have our daily choice of newspapers limited, because they have to make a conscious choice between offensive and non-offensive material.

People who want *porn* (for that *is* what these pictures amount to), should pay for it separately by buying the magazines that specifically cater for it. (They are despicable in themselves, but at least they are not foisted on to people who do not want them.) By printing these pictures in *news*papers, people buying them for *news* are having offensive and distasteful material foisted on them in the process.

It is often said that these pictures are not offensive. People saying these things are likely to be the models themselves or someone connected with the newspaper – both of whom are making pots of money out of this *prostitution* – or men who obviously have to defend their source of a cheap and nasty thrill.

I do not believe there has *ever* been any justification for these *indecent* pictures to be printed in our *news*papers. The only purpose they serve for the paper is to sell more copies, and this means two things:

a)   A paper that relies on these pictures to boost their sales can't be much of a *news*paper. (A paper frightened of the effect *not* having these pictures in would lead to, probably ought not to be trading under the guise of a *news*paper at all.)

b)   There are obviously people buying these papers *primarily* because they are a source of regular and cheap porn. If the pictures weren't in them, they would either not be so particular about which papers they bought (as they would all be supplying the same commodity – ie, pure news) or they would cease buying a newspaper at all.

I do not believe boosting the sales of newspapers and keeping a proportion of the male population 'thrilled' is sufficient justification to keep these pictures in print. They *offend me*. Are *my* feelings not to be considered also?

That they excite and incite a large proportion of the male population cannot be denied – and in my view that is good enough reason to see these pictures banned from the press.

MANCHESTER

This letter, addressed to Joe Ashton, MP for Bassetlaw, is printed in its entirety in this section because it comes from a women's group which monitors the media.

I AM A member of Luton Women's Action Group. Part of our job is to monitor the media. One of our more unpleasant tasks is to occasionally buy *The Sun* and *The Star*, just to read what is being said about women.

The women of our group were horrified to see that a Labour MP is now writing for the gutter press, notorious for its racism and sexism, amongst other things. I support the Labour party, as do most of the women in the feminist movement, because we hope that through the Labour movement, our own second-class position will be greatly improved. However, some Labour men seem totally unaware, or uncaring about the real needs of women.

Your article* about Clare Short's proposal, seemed to miss the point entirely as to the real harm done by the tone of newspapers like *The Star* and *The Sun* especially the 'come and molest me' poses of the Page 3 girls (they are indeed girls, very young and impressionable girls . . .).

You say in your article that you never saw a real live naked woman until you went to a tatty touring show (tatty is your word) at the age of 12. I am surprised that you never saw your mother, or sisters, if you have any. Perhaps this explains why you don't understand women as people. You had as a child never seen a

* Joe Ashton, in his regular column for *The Daily Star* – 'Voice of the People' – wrote a piece on 13 March 1986 entitled 'Here's Why a Ban on Bare Boobs Wouldn't Cut the Rape Rate'. *The Star* (now Express Newspapers) would not give us permission to reproduce the column here, but in it Joe Ashton said that naked women had been cheering up the mundanities of life for years and the presence and availability of photographs of semi-naked women had no correlation to rape figures. He talked of the necessity to show 'impressionable young blokes' that pin-ups are for fun but 'the sentences on Page 1 are for real'. Suprisingly, Joe Ashton voted in favour of Clare Short's Indecent Displays Bill the second time round . . .

naked woman in a natural context, like home, or the beach. You say you have worked in sweaty jobs where the only 'ray of sunshine' is a bikini on a beach (you don't even say woman – she is just a bikini to you). Well, the world's most monotonous jobs are done mainly by women, who don't get much chance to ogle men's private parts. No, they are kept well covered by the male controlled media, on the whole.

You say the first bloke who learned to chisel on the walls of caves carved pictures of topless women. How amusing that this is what you think, when you don't even know for certain that it was men who did the artwork. Perhaps you think women are incapable of drawing. Anyway, most of the cave drawings I have seen are of bison etc. And topless women wouldn't have raised an eyebrow, as they were all fairly naked in those days, even the men weren't covered up from head to toe as they are now, you know.

You say that Page 3 doesn't encourage men to commit rape any more than looking at pictures of supermarket sausages will lead to more shoplifting. Well, advertising does actually lead to more shoplifting, as it is there to encourage (and titillate) people to buy more goods. And if they can't afford the goods, what do they often do? Shoplift, of course.

Yes, I agree that men who produce newspapers do not understand a lot about women's dignity. That point I do agree with wholeheartedly. But then you say it is because as young lads you are all trained to jump in the same rugby bath or shower. Well, there's nothing humiliating about that. Girls are happy enough to be seen naked by other girls. You ought to see sisters getting ready to go out. They flit around from bedroom to bathroom in the nude, without a care, because they know they are in the safety of their own company, and aren't going to be appraising each other as sex objects.

You say that when you stand together at a urinal, you couldn't care less, but I have heard from several of my male family and acquaintances, that you find it quite hard to pee in front of even other men. (I wonder what you would do if a woman wandered into the urinal to have a good look and compare penises? But of course we are 'banned' from male urinals, because men don't want to be seen in that state of vulnerability by women – after all, we might laugh.) I wonder how you would cope with a bunch of women looking at your 'chipolatas' and 'bananas'? If you wouldn't mind, perhaps you would care to display your own Page 3, after all, they pay quite well, I hear. . . .

You say that men can't convince women that pin-ups don't lead to rape. I wonder why? Perhaps it is because we are the ones who experience threats from men every day of our lives. We have to be careful even when we go out in the evening, in case we are assaulted. You don't know what that feels like, so don't try to set yourself up to try and 'convince' women that they are wrong.

You say that if masturbatory fantasies aren't available, then sex-starved men are far more likely to take to the streets instead of the privacy of their own bedrooms. What are you saying about your own sex? Are you saying that men are not able to control themselves and live by reason, rather than emotions getting the better of them? Many have always told women that they are the reasonable sex, that it is women who get emotional. Yet women don't have masturbatory fancies provided for them, they don't generally have male pin-ups at work, yet they do not go out and rape young boys. And men in some parts of the world (so called primitive societies) do not rape women, neither do they have masturbatory fancies of Page 3 in the privacy of their huts. These men exhibit the so called 'feminine' qualities of caring and tenderness, and they are taught to respect the women, who are quite highly thought of in their own communities. We women know that Page 3 is much more about the power men want over women than real sex urges. Men commit rape because they are inadequate enough to want power over someone less powerful than them. When women are treated with more respect by the media, then men will treat them with more respect. Heavy sentencing may demonstrate that society frowns on rape, but it does not reform a rapist.

Please don't confuse Samantha Fox with the Venus de Milo.* The context is very different. Male and female nudes have always been portrayed in art, and not always for pornographic purposes. You say yourself that Page 3 is for masturbatory fancies. Are you saying that Venus de Milo is sculpted for the purpose of arousing these fantasies? Some nudes are simply aesthetically pleasing. The body is a beautiful form, both male and female. But poor Samantha Fox and her colleagues are photographed in a way which is suggestive and provocative. When the sculptors of the early church worked on statues of Mary, the mother of Jesus, they first sculpted her in the nude. The original sculptures were totally pure, and very unprovocative (unless they provoked men into saying their prayers). So the context is very important. Women on the beach are behaving as any normal human being would, they are not posing to titillate men, they are stripping off for the

---

* Confusing nudity with pornography, Ashton said that 'banning Samantha Fox in colour or draping a gown over Venus de Milo in an art gallery would not stop the rise in violent crime figures'.

feel of the sun on their bare flesh. Early goddesses were sculpted in the nude, and men fell down in awe, not lust. I would suggest that if breasts suddenly became a symbol of female power men would hate the sight of them. They are, after all, designed for feeding babies. They should be a very powerful symbol of women's ability to give birth. A lot of men don't think that it is right for a woman to feed a baby in public, yet they think Page 3 is fine, because it is there not as a symbol of women's power, but as a symbol of their own power.

Men don't want to lose this power (many of them – not all), so they will of course object when some 'spoilsport' woman MP tries to take away one of their power privileges.

LUTON

Danger – Men at Work

Pornography in the Workplace

The difficulty for women in exercising their freedom not to look at pornography so obviously displayed in most newsagents is dealt with in Chapter 7. These letters specifically address the ways in which tabloid pornography affects women's experience at work. Its acceptability in the workplace, where other forms of pornography might not be tolerated, functions as a tacit social understanding that women still exist for the pleasure of men, whatever their occupation or profession and that their efficiency in this task will always be more important than their skill or efficiency at their job.

Women wrote in representing dozens of jobs and professions – teachers, sales staff, TV producers, secretaries, nurses, barristers, factory workers, policewomen and scientists. Sexual harassment, condoned by these newspapers, was present in all these workplaces. If it's in the newspapers, it must be OK. OK to put pin-ups and calendars on the wall, OK to comment on a woman's looks or appearance above all else, OK not to take her very seriously at all.

The presence of Page 3 pictures or calendars puts obstacles in the way of women right through the employment process from interview to promotion. Women who complain not only risk a barrage of insults but risk being labelled as a troublemaker. Women's objections are often dismissed. They are mocked or silenced into feeling that their complaint has nothing to do with asserting their own rights and everything to do with messing up the joke and the fun of the boys. It's just a laugh/it brightens up the day/don't be a spoilsport. Their treatment when they object to the presence of nudity shows that women have a long way to go before they are truly accepted and integrated into the workforce. As some of these letters show, voicing a grievance can even result in violent behaviour. Even though some companies and unions have introduced policies and procedures regarding sexual harassment at work, they often fail to recognise the links between this behaviour and pin-up pictures. It still falls to individual women to initiate a complaint and it is only when these women are in positions of authority themselves that realistic measures are guaranteed.*

People have very little control over who they work with. They cannot choose their workmates in the same way they choose their friends. For women this puts them at a double disadvantage since they are often in a minority in the workplace anyway. The existence of a pin-up calendar or Page 3 on a staff room wall disrupts any possible equality between male and female colleagues before working relationships have even begun to develop by presenting women as public property to men they don't know. How fair can the delineation of working rights be given that men have already claimed that shared public space, and the women in it, as their own. Think of the particular predicament of the many women working in newsagents, who are forced as part of their job to handle, display and sell pornographic material.

From these letters one can see very clearly the way in which pornography in the workplace is used by men to keep women in the place they would like them, which is not where they might challenge men for jobs or promotion. Some men simply cannot see the politics behind their pinning up of pictures or even their tacit tolerance of them, but wherever it exists it shows women that they are not welcome, or that they are only welcome as long as they play the game, dress to please, laugh in the right places and don't get ideas above their subordinate station.

Britain's workforce needs women. By 1995, for example, it is estimated that 80% of the necessary increase in the workforce will have to come from the ranks of women.† At a time when initiatives are being taken to encourage women returners to fill the gaps in industry, women have little evidence that their interests are being represented or noted at work. Women must be made to feel an integral part of the workforce and that their economic presence is not just regarded as an expedient measure when there are not enough men to do the work required, but as one of society's general requirements. This is not just a matter of tacking the odd creche onto existing work structures, but re-evaluating and adapting those structures in ways which make them more flexible and responsive to the needs of women.

Images of women at work frequently appear in pornography which endorses the myth that despite the uniform – or the status – all women are seduceable: nurses (beds and bedpans), teachers

* In April 1990, the GPO banned pin-ups in its offices after a survey revealed that hundreds of women in senior positions had experienced sexual harassment.
† BPIF/NGA/SOGAT Booklet, June 1990.

(private lessons and spankings), lawyers (sentencing and punishments). The sexualisation of these jobs bears little relation to their day to day reality and undermines the contribution of women in these socially important occupations. Moreover the concept of a working woman is ritually ridiculed by the pornographic representation of these women in tabloids.

That men are very protective of their power and their right to control public spaces was clearly seen in the way male MPs treated Clare Short in her workplace when she tried to challenge this right. Refusing to see the issue of Page 3 in its proper political context, they reacted primarily as men with the instinctive bullying tactics of a territorial show. Respecting the public presence of women and taking the nude pictures out of the papers was seen as a measure designed to hinder a small male pleasure, as Robert Adley claimed in the debate. The cries of spoilsport hung in the air and the principles behind the 'complaint' were never fully debated.

Clare Short's treatment in the House of Commons reflected for many their own treatment at work. It struck such a chord of empathy and despair. Here was a woman at the top of her profession attempting to do her job and being belittled and dismissed. So many women had felt that it was just their cross to bear and that they were being oversensitive but witnessing Clare Short's treatment made them realise that their experiences were not different and that this institutional harassment is common to all women, whoever they are, wherever they work.

LAST THURSDAY, ONE of my workmates (who are all men) expressed great indignation about a recent rape case, and went on at great length about how all rapists should be hung. I pointed out that he was viewing it from only one end of the scale and so long as Page 3 and such pornographic material is widely accepted and condoned, male children will grow up with attitudes to sex that lead to women being raped. I was working hard to get him and my other workmates to see the connections when over the radio came a voice saying exactly the same thing. That was the first I heard of your proposed bill, so of course I was very pleased.

The only thing I regret is that the Bill cannot be extended to cover nude calendars, such as are seen in garages and offices and magazines such as *Playboy* which are on view in W.H. Smiths and most newsagents. I am not saying the magazines should be banned – just that they should not be on display where children can see them, and they are offensive to many women.

DERBY

PICTURES OF NUDE women in daily 'newspapers' are humiliating and degrading to women. *Well done* in introducing your bill banning their inclusion in newspapers. I asked a friend who works in W.H. Smiths what she felt about having to sell papers like *The Sun* and sex magazines. She doesn't like it at all, but has to because it is her job . . .

TOWN WITHHELD

I AM 19 and work with a lot of women and girls who *all* agreed with you – in fact I think most women in this country are in agreement but they are afraid of being called 'prudes'. I am sure you will have a lot of opposition from the men of the country and also the Page 3 girls themselves, who make so much money out of posing. They say the only people who object to them are dowdy women with flat chests. Not so. The girls here are all well endowed and attractive, but are sick of the exploitation and the comments a lot of us get from men who work here like, 'Go on, show us your Page 3s' or 'She's got a big pair' and 'give us a flash'. We are respectable girls who like to look nice without being degraded.

TOWN WITHHELD

I AM A woman shop steward and I work in a large factory. Until recently we had to put up with pictures of naked or half-naked women pasted up all over the place. After the women got together and made one hell of a fuss the *male* supervisor had them all taken down. The funny thing is that when one of my women friends got a picture of a naked man and pinned it over her locker the men didn't like it. They said it was vulgar and pornographic. We get fed up with the snide remarks from the men about the size of our personal assets as compared to Page 3 girls and seeing the supposedly grown up, civilised men drooling and giggling over the pictures like this. When I ask some of the men if they would put the nude calendars up in their own living rooms, they said they certainly wouldn't. Well, if their wives won't put up with pornography at home, I won't put up with it at work.

HULL

THREE YEARS AGO when I worked in a large open-plan office, the men delighted in hanging up a Page 3 calendar and, as I was the only one who objected, there it remained. If customers came on the floor where I worked, it would have had to be removed but because I was the only one offended, it stayed put. I wish I had made a search for a nude male calendar and waited to see what the management thought of that. Of course, you are always called a killjoy and some even say you're jealous – to which I assure them that 20 years ago, my figure was just as voluptuous but I chose to earn my living typing rather than degrade my sex. I think you're tough enough to take all the criticism on the chin if you remember that so many ordinary women like me are on your side.

SHEFFIELD

FOR MANY YEARS I worked mainly with men, as my job was male-dominated, and breaktimes were always acutely embarrassing with comments being made on the latest Page 3 offering. It never became any less embarrassing with time. Surely, it is as much a part of sexual harassment for many British women as any other offensive and unwanted sexual comment, 'groping', innuendo, etc. So only one good reason out of many for banning newspaper nudes would be to remove one particular cause of alienation and harassment from the lives of working (and all) women.

BRISTOL

I HAVE WORKED as a lab technician since the mid 1960s but, because of the present economic situation, have not had a permanent job since 1981. Last year I got a temporary job in the lab of a local factory. I was absolutely horrified by the attitude of the male workers to me and the other woman in the lab – that all women were shit and should be treated as shit. (I'm sorry if that sounds offensive but there is no milder way to accurately express it.) This was, of course, worse among the younger men on the factory floor who had never in their adult lives read anything but tabloid newspapers, but the tendency was spreading among the older men and those who were so-called educated/executive.

I have not had a particularly sheltered life – bad language and outspoken sexual comment seem to have always been regarded as acceptable in the scientific fraternity, and in the early 1970s I worked in factory labs where some of the men I dealt with were very tough indeed – but I was utterly shocked by the change in attitude of men to women that has taken place in the last few years.

CHESHIRE

I'M SURE THE newspapers are often bought instead of 'girlie' magazines. I am a solicitor and on one occasion in court while waiting for a verdict (the judge and the jury having retired) I noticed one of the barristers getting out *The Sun* and passing it round for his colleagues to look at Page 3. I voiced my objections which were treated with surprise . . .

TOWN WITHHELD

I WORK IN an office of mixed sexes and I am sick and tired of seeing these pictures from newspapers bandied about for all interested parties to have an ogle, snigger and leer at. To me, not only are the pictures offensive but also the behaviour they lead to in people I work with; behaviour which I am 'forced' to grin and bear in order to keep the peace in what is otherwise a pleasant office to work.

MANCHESTER

I AGREE WITH you, there must be a link between Page 3 – and the Page 3 mentality which seems to guide much of the editorial of *The Sun* et al – and the frightening rise in horrifying sexual crimes against both women and children. I personally have been subjected to sexual harassment at work. I was forced into a corner away from my colleagues and asked if I looked like the Page 3 girl thrust under my nose. I have been followed and pestered on dark evenings on my way home from work – twice. I am an ordinary looking 29-year-old married woman and bear little resemblance to a Page 3 girl. My experience is the same, or milder, than that of thousands of others.

LONDON

AS A TEACHER in a comprehensive school, I often hear the degrading comments about women made by adolescent boys and, so often, there is a comment about Page 3 girls. Recently, a 16-year-old boy got out his *The Sun* newspaper with the comment 'There's a picture of you in here, Miss'. It was Samantha Fox, to whom I bear no more of a resemblance than having longish fair hair. I realised that such pictures encourage disrespect of women in authority by reducing them all to no more than naked bodies. However, it is the effect it has on the whole female population that most concerns me. I fear that until we achieve a higher percentage of women MPs, we will be dismissed as 'spoilsports' and 'jealous, ugly old bats' etc, etc. Please let me know if there are any positive steps I could take to ensure that no woman ever again has to suffer the agony of rape because of the gutter press's unhealthy greed for greater profits.

GLOUCESTER

SADLY, IT DOES not surprise me that you had to persevere through laughter and jeers from other members of the House of Commons – no doubt they were men. I don't think it will ever be possible to *prove* a link with sexual violence against women, but it is clear that these photographs represent all women as sexual targets for males. Many men would deny this happens but my experiences show how these photographs label all women as 'sex objects'.

I work as a police officer, where the ratio is 10:1 men to women.

I dread the arrival of the morning papers. A crowd forms to view 'Page 3' or 'Page 7'. I will spare you a recital of the lewd comments that follow – it seems to make them even happier if a woman police officer is in the room to be humiliated by their ribaldry. 'It's only a bit of fun, isn't it?' I used to think I was respected by my colleagues until one day when a group of them were viewing Page 3 a sergeant said to me 'Are your tits like this?' I knew then that I would never be an equal to him in his view but only a potential sex object.

TOWN WITHHELD

HAVING SPENT FIVE years in the police force, I had become quite used to sexist put-downs but assumed that to be an occupational hazard. It was when I heard the reactions of men like Adley that I realised the full significance of the Page 3 issue. Why did such educated men react in this way? I can only imagine that Page 3 is recognised as one of the ways of keeping women 'in their place'. If our elected representatives feel this is necessary then I feel they can go to hell – figuratively . . .

TOWN WITHHELD

RECENTLY, I CHANGED my job when the men where I worked continually put up Page 3 girls as a way of showing how little my presence was welcomed. When I complained I received little sympathy, for I was seen as having provoked them to it by getting angry when they constantly talked of women in an obscene and disrespectful way.

TOWN WITHHELD

I – A YOUNG, attractive, blonde female – used to share an office with five men, I being the only woman. One of these men put up topless calendars and pin-ups. When I finally objected, it turned out that none of the other men particularly liked these pictures and, in fact, were rather embarrassed by them – however, it wasn't done for men to object! The reaction from the man concerned, however, was violent. This, I believe, typifies attitudes towards pin-ups. I believe only a minority actually like them. Most women don't wish to object because they are afraid they will appear jealous, prudish, frigid, old-fashioned etc, etc. Men don't tend to object because it isn't 'macho' to object (although I believe most of them are rather embarrassed at these kind of pictures – or at least indifferent). However, since the men who like these pictures can be so hysterical in defence, one has to feel strongly to brave the reaction by daring to complain. Most, for a quiet life, put up and shut up. Indeed after a tantrum from my Page 3-loving colleague, I said no more about his calendars and they stayed, though I could easily have made him take them down. I did not want to make a fuss and have people think I was straightlaced or anything.

Actually the man concerned was physically grotty and had been making passes at me nonstop so accusations of jealousy would be ridiculous but nevertheless they would be made.

BIRMINGHAM

AT ONE TIME I had a job as a junior member of staff in a factory where all the other staff members were men. It was a common experience to go into an office and find men admiring the latest Page 3 girl. This continuous and everyday experience of women being degraded definitely made my task of persuading the other staff members to take me at all seriously even more difficult. I was very sorry that you were subject to such appalling treatment by Tory MPs and feel that you deserve an apology. I am writing to Mrs Thatcher to tell her so.

TOWN WITHHELD

I WAS INTERVIEWED for a job once and was really put off by the large picture of a Page 3 nude hanging on the wall. The man who was conducting the interview kept looking first at me, then at the pin-up. I got the job but would not accept it – he really made my blood boil. I was also livid when the MPs scoffed at your bill; surely they must take notice now. You were so courageous, Clare – it must have been awful for you, but you are not alone. It's time women spoke up and thank goodness we have someone like you to fight for us. What I cannot understand is why the Prime Minister hasn't done more – after all, she is a woman too. I have written to several MPs and various magazines in the hope that this will do something to help the ban. I can understand how jubilant you felt when you knew that the (*Woman*) report was on your side.* When I read it, I felt like celebrating. I thought 'At last – something might be done'.

TOWN WITHHELD

LIKE SO MANY, I was disgusted and hurt when I heard the behaviour of certain MPs in response to your Bill – ironically, of course, that male jeering underpinned the validity of what you were saying to perfection – but when even privileged and educated men show so unashamedly their contempt for the feelings of women, what hope can there be for the rest?

Working in television, I feel doubly frustrated. Here too, I am surrounded by able and intelligent men with the ability to take a stand on a matter like this but who consistently refuse to do so. Even the simplest protest meets with scorn, and suggestions that one must be a lesbian, frigid, or jealous of other women – all three possibilities (revealingly enough) deemed to be so damning that no further discussion need occur! The saddest aspect to me of this sort of schoolboy reaction is that even young men have it – the new generation whom we had hoped would grow up to know better.

More important than this, however, is the distressing disregard of some programme makers towards a careful, and caring, treatment of women. There have, recently, been two prime examples of this, one on each BBC channel and each, by chance, concerning Samantha Fox. On Joan Rivers's *Can We Talk?* Miss Fox walked on to the strains of 'I've got a lovely bunch of coconuts'. On *Pebble Mill at One*, after the same young woman had sung her current hit (and in my opinion it will be a long time before we'll hear anything more inciting to rape than this horribly successful effort!) gyrating around an aircraft carrier among

* Following Clare Short's attempt to introduce her Bill, *Woman* magazine published the results of a survey which showed how their readers felt about Page 3. Over 5000 readers responded, of which a staggering 90% wanted Page 3 to be banned. 4 out of 5 also believed that these pictures were linked with crimes against women (see *Woman*, 30 August 1986).

sailors and torpedoes, the presenter referred to her as 'all ship shape and Bristol fashion'.*

At the moment, there is still nothing that women television professionals can do, and I fear that this will not change until more women are present, as Department Heads, at programme review. All I can do is look after my own programmes, bring up my son to value women in an honest manner and offer you my sincerest good wishes.

TOWN WITHHELD

GENERALLY, I AM inclined to close my eyes to what I do not like, but even I am shaken from my lethargy by the obvious link between naked women and abuse. Yet, I could not be lethargic as a nurse at University College. I had to ensure that I travelled, not in my uniform, but in anonymous clothes. The image of 'Naughty Nurse Nita' is pervasive. If that is my experience, how much worse is it for school children.

TOWN WITHHELD

I, LIKE MANY other women, am concerned over the increasing violence that is directed to women in the home, on the streets and in the workplace. There is no doubt in my mind that the way the media, in particular the popular press, present women is at least a contributory factor.

It is a sad reflection on women's purported value in society, that they have few opportunities to earn the wages available to them for taking their clothes off. Certainly, working long antisocial shifts as a nurse, for example, doesn't command such a fee.

TOWN WITHHELD

SOME TIME AGO, I worked as Art Director for a pornographic magazine, which was something I was able to justify to myself that it was the girls who exploited themselves. Whether from

* Samantha Fox's 'Touch Me' reached Number 3 in the UK Pop Charts in 1986.

greed or vanity, it was their choice and not something that morally affected anyone else. In addition, the models were often paid large sums of money, unlike the dozens of exhibitionists who were rushing to display themselves for no benefit or payment on the Readers' Wives/Girlfriends/Daughters pages of rival magazines. I was aware, certainly, of the existence of immense misogyny in our society but considered that to be the produce of sick minds, not something that would be particularly fostered by photographs of nude women.

Since those days, my opinions have changed radically, particularly after reading *Women Against Violence Against Women* – a book that Edwina Currie might benefit from reading – which draws clear and powerful arguments for banning a number of things which are widely accepted and legally permitted in our society.*

The presentation of women as provocative and available in such widely accessible media such as newspapers, even at tabloid level, are highly damaging to women as a whole. Women will be damaged in their own eyes if they do not 'match-up'; they will be damaged in the future views of their children who will grow up to see women valued only for their sexual attractiveness and objectified status in our so-called equal society. Please continue in your fight which offers hope for a kinder presentation of women in the future.

LONDON

* *Women Against Violence Against Women* edited by dusty rhodes and Sandra McNeill, Onlywomen Press, 1985. It is a collection of essays on the different types of violence affecting women's lives.

Rights of Way

Women and Public Transport

Robert Adley's amused reference to *The Sun* readers on the tube provoked an angry response. Women corrected his interpretation of this phenomenon as a small pleasure and informed him of the discomfort, humiliation, embarrassment and sheer terror that can accompany a woman as she travels on buses, trains and tubes as a matter of course, let alone in the company of men enjoying pornography.

Illustrations of the price women pay in order to preserve this male right to ogle in public ranged from the way men will look at a woman to comments, threats and actual physical assaults. All of which make it impossible for a woman to take for granted *at any time* her freedom to travel without exercising varying degrees of caution.

Many people read their papers on the way to work giving this material a very public airing and daily it is tolerated in cramped shared spaces. Yet, with every furtive underground grope or leer, early morning male fantasies become a grim reality for women who are forced to travel in close proximity to men they don't know.

Women especially rely on train and bus networks in order to protect their independence of movement. Taxis can be prohibitively expensive and in any case, many women still do not feel comfortable about getting in to what is, after all, a strange man's car. Women speak of not wanting to be reliant on husbands and boyfriends for lifts to and from their destinations and many a woman forced in to this position would rather not go out than presume upon a man's generosity.

While long waits, staff cutbacks and badly-lit carriages and stations are unpleasant for everyone, they constitute a very real threat for women. Women do not feel safe using public transport at night or on their own and this is not the result of paranoia or scaremongering but the product of their experience. This experience has never been fully incorporated in the planning of our transport systems. Even installation of surveillance equipment has more to do with staffing levels than consideration for women travellers. Closed circuit cameras will never provide the reassurance that a well-staffed station does.*

Recent crime statistics show a huge increase in sexual assaults, increasing a woman's fear as she travels around.† Guidelines are issued and reissued for women who travel: don't get into empty carriages, walk opposite oncoming traffic, adopt body language to deter someone from approaching. It is always the woman who must take the preventative measure and exercise caution. Never in these survival kits is the issue of socially acceptable porn on public transport dealt with. Never is the part it plays in the constant harassment and assault of women recognised. Because when it comes to men taking preventative action, the daily experience of women is denied.

The glib remarks of Robert Adley and his dubious pleasures are a sad reminder of this. They are simply not funny. These letters reflect the fear and frustration women feel when travelling with men. Their's is a completely different experience. We might be in the same carriage as Mr Adley, but we are worlds apart.

I OVERHEARD TWO 9-year-old boys the other day on the bus talking about the size of the woman's breasts they had seen in *The Sun* the day before, referring to the woman as an object: 'You should have seen the tits on it!' These young children had no qualms about this treatment and depiction of women. Why should they? Society condones this attitude everywhere.

Videos and magazines depict violence against women as enjoyable to the woman. I find this terrible as I know the fear and loathe male violence and see so many men looking at me with the

---

* On 26 October 1989, *The Evening Standard* reported that British Rail was to replace staff with ticket barriers and closed circuit cameras on Southern Region stations at off-peak times. This on a line where 14 rapes had occurred in the previous five years, despite British Rail claiming that they were concerned about providing a 'safer travelling environment'. But they did increase the number of ticket inspectors to cut down on ticket fraud.

† 'Criminal Statistics England and Wales 1989'; the Home Office. These figures show a three-fold increase in reported rapes since 1979.

Star Bird still in his head; seeing me as ready, well-equipped and willing to fulfil his wildest fantasies.

LANCASHIRE

DEAR MR ADLEY, I can understand your pleasure in watching the face of a man pretending not to look at Page 3 on the underground train. That pleasure would turn to extreme embarrassment, discomfort and humiliation when the man, a complete stranger, looked up and you knew from the look on his face that he had mentally undressed you. I really don't think you can honestly understand how very unpleasant that can be, since I am quite sure it has never happened to you, and it is certainly not a compliment. Is your pleasure worth that cost? It happens to women of all ages, every day, everywhere in Great Britain, and if you don't believe me, ask your wife or your secretary.

DORSET

IT'S DISGRACEFUL – THOUGH sadly predictable – that a House full of *men* should ridicule your attempts to prevent the sexual harassment and abuse of women, and depressing that they have the power to block your demands. It may be amusing for a *man* to watch another man looking at Page 3, but for a *woman* sharing the same carriage, it can be both humiliating and intimidating. The sooner people realise the connection between pornography and rape, the sooner something will be done to prevent such terrible violations of our freedom and ourselves. As long as women's bodies are used casually or disrespectfully by the media and by advertising, we will be encouraging men to do likewise.

TOWN WITHHELD

PAGE 3 GIRLS, because of the huge fees they are allowed to extract, can become free from possible rape, as they can buy protection from attack, and live in areas reasonably free from this kind of thing, and not have to find themselves using public transport, or even having to walk the last few hundred yards from the bus stop at night in the dark, yet they happily perform in their poses in Murdoch's and Maxwell's rags and comics, and men really do, we believe, begin to think all women, if they are not, ought to be, like the people in these pictures, or have something wrong with them.

TOWN WITHHELD

IF YOU EVER have the misfortune to speak to the moron who talked about the pleasures of being on a tube train full of *The Sun* readers, you might tell him that ordinary women like me find it both offensive and distressing to sit on a train and be confronted by degrading images of women.

I recently suffered a 20 minute train journey with a photo of a bare breasted Linda Lusardi thrust into my face. I spent the journey trying to decide whether or not I should speak up and tell the offending male reader how I felt, but was finally too intimidated by the presence of many other male tabloid readers in the carriage. I was left feeling angry at my own cowardice, but angrier at the tactic intimidation these tawdry images can cause in women.

TOWN WITHHELD

I TRAVEL DAILY on the tube to north London. For much of the distance I am alone in the carriage or with just one person as we go through empty stations – often a man 'reading' Page 3! How do I explain to this man, should it be necessary, that one explicit picture does not mean that all women's bodies are available for his amusement. We have recently heard too many judges pronounce attacks on women as 'sickening', 'horrifying' or 'degrading', without trying to understand the cause. If Page 3 pictures are in any way responsible we are all at risk if we let them continue.

LONDON

I HAVE OFTEN squirmed with discomfort when sitting on a train next to a man who has Page 3 of *The Sun* fully open next to me and, being aware of his intense gaze at the model, I wonder in what light he would see me if I were suddenly to ask him for the time (as men, strangely, seem to lump all women together).

ESSEX

I WAS UNFORTUNATE enough to travel home one evening in a carriage in the company of two 15 or 16-year-old boys pawing over a copy of *The Sun*. They repeatedly compared the picture to me – I ignored them. Later as I walked from the station to home, they jumped on me. Luckily, I managed to slash one of them along his arm (I won't say with what, it's illegal) – I ran and ran until safely at home. I have never told anyone this but if you wish to use it as evidence please do.

ESSEX

Not in Front of the Children

Educational Influences

Many women wrote as mothers worried for their families – sons developing false impressions, daughters trying to live up to them. They were outraged that Page 3, which they felt degraded women, was permitted to slip the censorship net and pass in to mainstream circulation where more explicit material had not. *The Sun*, *The Star* and *The Daily Mirror* are so-called 'family newspapers', freely available to *anyone* who wishes to purchase them.

Women wanted to challenge this smokescreen and register their anger that parental influences were being so blatantly undermined. Children are impressionable and quick to learn. Their behaviour indicates the priorities society teaches. Children can see what is held dear and what is rewarded; what is dismissed and what is despised. People are unwilling to accept the wider influences of the culture we have created but all these letters show how the family is not the sole protector and educator of children. Society clearly has a collective responsibility when it comes to the education of the nation's children.

Page 3 is often desperately defended on the grounds that it can fulfil a sex educational role by presenting things not talked about. In families where no educational material but this is available, girls will assume that their function in life is to please, titillate, be passive and to disregard their own needs. For girls, far from being a lesson in sex, it is a lesson in how to please a man in a man's world. Boys will assume their right to judge a woman in terms of her physical attributes. Tabloid sexuality is a reactionary education which does not encourage the young to define their own sexuality or to see the necessity of discovering the emotional needs of their partners.

The so-called naturality of Page 3 is often held to be an open and frank portrayal of the naked form. Accusations of prudery dismiss objections as being in some way Victorian and connected with taboo and inhibition. Women who wrote in did not object to their children being exposed to nudity and valued the open discussion of sexuality but they challenged the Page 3 definition of openness and the way in which it concentrated exclusively on women.

Children deliver papers such as *The Sun* and *The Sunday Sport*. They can see adults, who they are encouraged to respect and trust, reading them. They are used to cover the art tables in their schools. Their exposure means that the only step left to complete their involvement with its ethos is to buy it – a small step, but a significant one so far as the newspaper barons are concerned.

Page 3 girls are young. They are relatively thin, hairless and childlike. Sadly, this seems to have become something of an ideal. The effect is that women attempt to remain childlike. Not just breasts, but menstruation, body hair – these are the facts of women's sexuality, but when did you last see a Page 3 girl with unshaved armpits or a bikini line? If we are going to call these pictures natural, why are they so untrue to life? Why is body hair unacceptable in this country for women, given its natural state? Why do some men find childlike Page 3 *girls* more attractive than real *women*? And what more proof do we need to see the worrying links here with the sexual abuse of children?

MY HUSBAND AND I are both psychiatric nurses and, as such, well aware of the 'black stocking and easy virtue' portrayal of the nursing profession in Page 3 of *The Sun*, *The Sunday Sport* and *The News of the World*. As a woman I find this kind of picture deeply offensive, and do feel it helps portray women as easily available to be used and abused by men.

We have a 2-year-old child, a daughter, who we are consciously trying to bring up in a non-sexist way. We encourage her to be proud of her body and confident in herself and her abilities. We will find it very difficult to explain to her why semi- clad women are printed in provocative poses in so-called newspapers. Newspapers should contain news, not pornography.

LINCOLNSHIRE

AS A TEACHER of adolescents, I am always trying to encourage the boys to take the girls seriously, and the girls to take *themselves* seriously. It is very difficult to do this faced with a barrage of tits and bums in the daily papers. It is also worth noting that girls frequently (and maybe subconsciously) compare their looks and figures with the models in the tabloids. Finding that they do not 'match up' can cause all sorts of problems, from lack of self-esteem to compulsive eating and anorexia.

TOWN WITHHELD

I WAS APPALLED to hear an excerpt of a debate in the House last week in which male members (who outnumber women MPs shamefully) treated your commonsense remarks so contemptuously. I wonder if they realised how many women *voters*, listening to their jeers, would be angered and frustrated? While the question of the media's presentation of women is treated in this nudge-nudge, giggly fashion, how can we hope to establish equality of opportunity for women and restraint on the part of the male?

Before I became a full-time mother, I taught English in several secondary schools. I'm completely accustomed to the coy, excited sniggers of second year boys when papers are discussed and Page 3 of *The Sun* is invariably mentioned by somebody. Little did I expect to catch the selfsame reaction in grown men who presume to legislate on behalf of my husband, my children and myself! I have had ample opportunities over the last eight years to see how quickly young children absorb and copy the (often unspoken) attitudes of people, stories and pictures around them.

TOWN WITHHELD

BOYS – STUPID BOYS of course – start sniggering about girls in school and sapping their confidence by the time they are 13. Now, would boys behave like that if Page 3 was not on their breakfast tables every morning? Real pornography takes some obtaining – it is Page 3 which is the pervasive, pernicious influence.

WILTSHIRE

AS AN INFANT school teacher, it always upset me when the children spread out newspapers (brought in by helpful parents) and there was a pouting naked woman between the paint pots. The little boys would snigger, and the little girls would look at them and look at me, wondering if they should snigger too – their faces full of perplexity and unease.

NORTHAMPTONSHIRE

BEFORE TAKING A craft lesson with a class of 10/11 year olds, I suggested that the desks should be protected with newspaper. One bright spark started a scrum to find every Page 3 for his desk and after the lesson was over, an embarrassed little girl brought me cut-out nipples which had dropped to the floor. This was a minute and short-lived incident, but it angered me that the possibility for it to take place existed.

YORKSHIRE

I AM THE mother of a one-year-old girl, and I am appalled to think that, unless you are successful, she will grow up in a society where the female body is considered public property and women regarded first as the bearers of 'tits' rather than as thinking people with a right to be private about their 'tits' and other sexual parts if they so wish. As matters stand now, her male peers (as well as older men) will definitely judge her as such. Worse, she may even begin to judge herself in the same, desperately inappropriate way.

Although I haven't expressed myself as well as I would have liked in this letter, I hope it (and the many others you must surely be receiving) will help keep your spirits up amidst the schoolboy jeers of other members of the house.

TOWN WITHHELD

I AM A teacher and I am aware that papers such as *The Sun* provide the first reading material, apart from school library books, for children as young as six. In many homes, these papers will be the only reading material available, and it distresses me that I am spending my life teaching children to read, just to give them access to this degrading rubbish.

BIRMINGHAM

CHILDREN TAKE THEM [newspapers] into school to cover up the desks in art which causes a lot of tittering and sniggering and when a 9-year-old boy started bringing in these photos to school and making suggestive remarks to the girls, well, I thought this was just the limit.

TOWN WITHHELD

MY 10-YEAR-OLD son has been chuckling over his knowledge of Page 3 'lovelies' for at least three years. I doubt that he's seen many copies but hears all about the 'latest' from friends at school. This is part of their daily diet which, at 7 years or less, they are not in a position to understand in any other context except 'tits and bums' – up for grabs if you can get 'em. To scrap all our Page 3s would be a small step in the direction of treating women, publicly at least, with the respect they deserve.

HUDDERSFIELD

WHY SHOULD MY son, for instance, on the one hand be told to respect women and then on the other, open a newspaper only to find a picture of a female purporting to have very little to offer except sex.

TOWN WITHHELD

HOW DO I explain to my 3-year-old daughter that this is the most lucrative way for a young girl to make money when I want her to grow up believing she is equal to men and can be a doctor, writer or scientist if she wants to?

TOWN WITHHELD

I SET MY daughters a personal example of modesty while answering their questions frankly, and am trying by the same method to instil in my son a healthy respect for womankind. All my efforts are undermined when he brings fish and chips home wrapped in someone's bare bosom.

TOWN WITHHELD

THE MOST WORRYING thing, to my mind, about these sorts of pin-ups is that they are accepted as normal by children who cannot fail to grow up with twisted, unbalanced views of male and female roles, both sexual and non-sexual. How can a little boy be expected to grow up believing people are people regardless of genitalia, with equal rights and potentials, when he is constantly confronted with the bizarre fact that the most important thing about women is that they have breasts? How can a little girl be expected to have the same hopes and expectations as her brother – aspire to be an engineer or a bank manager or a computer programmer – when she is constantly presented with role models of 'ideal women' whose mission in life is to please men? *All* men, including the ugly, smelly, down-and-out, stupid, socially incompetent – the Page 3 girl pushes her breasts at all of them and smiles invitingly.

WALES

MY SON IS a paper boy and when he first saw *The Sunday Sport* he began to read it obviously thinking it was about true sport. He says all the paper boys are reading it and that it's also doing the rounds at school. Do you agree that children should not be handling and delivering papers like this. Surely, they should be on the top shelf with the nude picture magazines?

TOWN WITHHELD

NO WONDER FEMALE (and male) children grow up confused: 'Don't go with strangers', 'This is taboo, that is taboo' etc, yet see Daddy leering at Page 3 and Mummy passively accepting to her,

her child's and all female body forms – plus the added insult to our intelligence when publishers and voyeurs attempt to pretend there is some kind of artistic merit to such pictures. Poppycock! It's plain titillation for the penises of the pathetic.

TOWN WITHHELD

I RECENTLY WROTE to the BBC about a children's presenter at 4 o'clock in the afternoon saying 'I met Sam Fox this afternoon,' (gasp while puppet falls back apparently overwhelmed) 'Nice lady, nice lady.' I objected to this admiration expressed at this time of a figure that I in no way would commend to my daughter of what women are and should be. This legitimation of such during children's television I FOUND APPALLING.

TOWN WITHHELD

IN MY MANY years of experience as an Art and Craft teacher, there were occasions when newspapers were brought into school to cover tables for practical work. They sometimes included semi-nude photographs and I was upset to see the coarse, contemptuous and sniggering reaction of some boys and the deep embarrassments of girls when these pictures came to light. It saddens me that these pictures have become so familiar in some households that the female body and persona are regarded with contemptuous indifference. It is tempting to see in this a development of callous attitudes which could so easily lead to an increase of exploitation and attacks on women.

SHROPSHIRE

ASSOCIATING SCHOOL UNIFORM for girls – even minimally – with nudity is surely extremely dangerous? The printing of the school reports gives the whole presentation a speciously acceptable flavour. Dads and brothers could be excused for having a glance and a smile. There are well-authenticated instances of girls being lain in wait for, and attacked, on their way home from school. *The*

Sun newspaper is not assisting in the struggle to enlighten the protagonists, and the general public, as to this genuine hazard.

EPSOM

TO SHOW TOPLESS schoolgirls is to invite perverts to suppose that young girls are fair sexual game. And this in a society where children have been lured from school playgrounds and sexually assaulted by men. What sort of a society allows a national daily newspaper to go this far?

HALIFAX

SOCIETY HAS BEEN turned into a playground for male sexuality, and people wonder why over the past 10 years sexual attacks have gone up by 40%. Sexual abuse against children is reaching an all time high. I'm quite sure this is no coincidence.

Food is advertised with mouthwatering pictures to make people hungry and go out and buy. Do men really get sexually stimulated and then forget about it? Or do a minority go out and rape or maybe satisfy themselves with some innocent child, who really asks nothing in return. I feel that some men may find the ever-ready naked female frightening and therefore, in his feelings of inadequacy, turn his attentions to a less threatening child.

Women are told from an early age that men find it difficult to control their sexual desires. Personally, I believe this is a lot of rot, but it serves as a fine excuse for the men who do not wish to control themselves. Much of the argument for the obsession with sex is that the public want it. Some of the public may want it, some of the public may also want to take drugs, rape, mug old people, slash up other human beings – are these things legal? Many of us also want jobs, decent housing, warmth in winter – do we get it?

At the age of 15, I became aware of the use of women in the media. I found it sickening; fifteen years on I still do. In my youthful mind, it occurred to me that many of the laws of censorship were changed as a form of candy for the masses, a sort of sweetener to keep them from thinking about more important things, but too much candy can eventually make a person's teeth rot and there are certainly a lot of things rotten in our society at the moment.

Well, Clare, I feel I've said enough at the moment in support of your fight, but I don't think it should stop there. How about men's magazines having plain covers as the variety of offensive pictures in local shops – breasts, bums, simulated masturbation – which adorn these magazines is totally unnecessary. We all know what is inside *Playboy* but I personally don't wish to see it.

TOWN WITHHELD

I AM A pupil at *W*— High School. We had a discussion in English about the Indecent Displays Bill and I quite agree with your views as did the majority in our class. I feel that women are degraded by these pictures in papers and magazines and I feel that until Page 3 is banned then some men will never learn not to treat women as mere 'sex objects'.

TOWN WITHHELD

I HAVE READ with interest the article about you in the May issue of *Everywoman* magazine.* When it was announced on Radio 1 last week that your Bill had not got through, I was sitting in the sixth form common room at school. Immediately, almost all the boys present started to talk over the radio so that we could not hear, saying things like 'It's all a big fuss about nothing. A pair of tits isn't going to make someone go out and rape a woman.' Ironically, one of the boys putting forward these views was someone that I had reported to a teacher for indecent exposure the previous term! It made me really angry, but I kept quiet and afterwards, I was glad that I had kept quiet, because if I start to argue for women's rights etc, when the other girls dare not say anything, one of those boys may guess that it was me that reported him. But, from the things I have heard girls say about it since then, I know that they are very glad that someone had the nerve to complain. I am pleased to know that you have had so many letters of support. One of the worst things about sexism is that women are often afraid to admit, even among themselves, that porn and

* *Everywoman*, May 1986.

sexual innuendoes do upset them, and making a big issue of Page 3 makes women feel more able to band together.

TOWN WITHHELD

I AM CONCERNED for the safety of my children – particularly my two girls, growing up in an increasingly violent society especially, it seems to me, a society that is increasingly contemptuous of the sexual privacy of women. It seems to me that the widespread publication in daily papers of semi-naked women must promote the 'subconscious' impression that

1) Women are universally sexually available.
2) It is women's purpose in life to titillate men.
3) It is this quality by which women are to be judged.

I feel that these pictures harm, or ignore, respect for women as people.

BIRMINGHAM

Smile Love, it Might Never Happen

Proving the Links

Those in power have a vested interest in preserving the status quo. Proof is demanded of the links between pornography and sexual violence. The idea that there must always be proof before something can be altered is a dangerous one as experience in other areas has shown. The drug Thalidomide was suspected to cause abnormalities but proof was demanded. By the time the proof had materialised, thousands of children had been born deformed.

When people talk of proof, they talk of statistics and evidence. On an issue like this 'proof' is hard to collate. It is often a woman's word against a man's and with his reputation and livelihood at stake, she has a hard case to prove. Women know only too well the way this society conducts a rape case and with what great licking of lips it is reported. Women often prefer to cope on their own with their experiences rather than consign them to the maverick systems by which we operate.

Society and its MPs should not insist that a woman be the victim of rape before she may be listened to. There is no hierarchy of abuse with 'victims' of rape at the top. All women's discomfort and humiliation should be taken seriously as well as the frustration and affrontery of 'non-victims'. Part of the reason MPs found it so easy to dismiss Clare Short's proposal was their unchallenged assertion in the House that she spoke only for herself and not for the women she claimed to represent. Women, incensed by this, wanted her to know what had happened to them.

Women related painful and intensely personal stories about the way porn made its unwelcome presence felt in their lives. That it was necessary for women to break their largely self-protective silence on this issue shows how strongly they felt about it and to what length they were prepared to go despite risks of being mocked or made to feel guilty. A woman reporting physical assault is forced to recount intimate details to one group of strangers after another, from police to lawyers to open court.

The links 'proved' by such evidence are highly subjective. Few women will claim that a particular Page 3 or pornographic picture incites men to rape. It is not simply a matter of proving that X Page 3 caused X attack, but in any case shouldn't the burden of proof be the other way round? Women's experience is their evidence. It is not good enough for men to say this evidence does not fit their methods. Their methods must be modified in order to include this experience.

Pornography *is* sexual violence. The abuse of countless women and children has taken place so that the material is available in the first place. It violates a woman's sexual freedom and privacy. It creates an atmosphere in which men feel they have rights as far as women are concerned – the right to see them, the right to comment upon them, the right to chase, to persist, ultimately to rape. The difference between a wolf whistle and an assault is huge but the difference between the attitudes that engender these actions is not.

Any woman will tell of the trepidation she feels when approaching a building site or a group of men – preparing herself for some kind of comment. Such advances are not made as one individual to another but as an act of bravado in a public place which embarrasses women and leaves them open to general assessment. It has little to do with the man feeling genuinely attracted to a woman and, even if it had, should he have the right to pass unsolicited judgement on a complete stranger?

The treatment of women as objects who look out of place if they are not smiling – 'Smile love, it might never happen' – is one that denies their individuality. The 'object' may have just lost a parent, a fiver or her patience. The constant demand on a woman's sociability and attractiveness in public is an offence in itself. As they go about their daily business, men are never asked to smile.

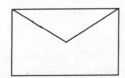

HOW CAN ANY civilised society have any self-respect when they shamelessly flaunt half-naked females over our daily newspapers to the affront of a large majority of that sex who are after all 51% of the population. I find it offensive, degrading, humiliating and a downright insult to my intelligence to have my gender represented at this base level alongside matters of national and universal concern.

It is difficult to conceive that there is no link between the drastic rise in sexual crime and the constant titillation we are deluged with every day whether we like it or not. Not to mention the way this undermines the female sex and continually reinforces her place as a second class citizen not to be taken seriously.

I am a community worker in Lambeth and see every day the sad effects of a society that undervalues such a large proportion of its population in this way . . .

LONDON

THE LINK BETWEEN rape and attitudes to women is, of course, difficult to prove (perhaps that depends on what is considered proof) but perhaps people would understand or accept a more insidious link. I am one of those women who as a child experienced what is now called 'child abuse', both brothers and my father pestered and molested me during my childhood, there were piles of mags under their beds which I think must have led to their feelings of what is appropriate behaviour towards girls and women.

TOWN WITHHELD

FROM EVERY POSSIBLE female point of view, these pictures are an abomination. I am now a granny but I have hated tham all my life. It seems common sense to me that if some men have their sexual desires continually aroused – and there can be no other purpose in these photographs – then those with what I call a low threshold of sexual self control will inevitably be pushed over the edge and lose their grip on that control. If the object of their original desire is not available to them then obviously they will look for a substitute. I am convinced that the high incidence of sexual crime bears a direct correlation to the higher incidence of commercial sexual stimulation. Any society with the smallest sense of responsibility must take steps to remove temptation, when the ones most likely to suffer as a result of it are those least able to protect themselves. My theory is unproven of course; it's just my instinct. What is not in doubt is that all women are degraded in the eyes of men by the few who allow themselves to be exploited in this way. All are held up to physical comparison and, no doubt, found inferior. The fact that a woman is a being with sensitivities, affections, ideas, intellect and spirit is entirely overlooked in the paradoxical exaltation/degradation of the merely physical. I strongly object to the fact that my granddaughter, my two daughters and myself are seen by some men as mounds of flesh, to be weighed up, assessed and savoured – or otherwise. Ugh . . .

TOWN WITHHELD

AS A FEMINIST and socialist and a victim of two rapes – and a victim of the continuous gibes all women are subjected to – I quite agree with you in thinking that these pictures degrade women and foster an attitude which germinates the seeds of rape. Rape is the violent and inevitable conclusion of women's position in society.

LONDON

AS A STUDENT here in Manchester, it is inhibiting to be a woman – girls have been raped at 5 and 6pm, so I and my friends would never go out alone after dark. The newspaper pictures certainly do not discourage men from being potential attackers and I know I speak for many fellow students who abhor this sexual harassment.

MANCHESTER

I WOULD LIKE to say that I support your campaign to ban Page 3 and semi-naked women's pictures that are spread all over the place. Eleven years ago I was sexually assaulted twice (once by my ex-boyfriend's stepdad, and two months later by 4 strangers as I walked alone). The people who support Page 3 pornography are very lucky they *do not suffer* the mental effect I get when faced with these pictures. I have recently been in touch with women from Rape Crisis, as I had to know why I find nudity or semi-nudity *unbearable* . . . these feelings are quite natural after the attacks. They say they know loads of women who feel exactly the same.

TOWN WITHHELD

CONSIDER HOW YOU might feel as a young woman in London, constantly experiencing harassment of one kind or another, unable to go out alone in the evenings, who from first hand experience knows the effect on men of the constant 'packaging' of women to suit their fantasies. It is not pleasant to feel constantly threatened and nervous, and it is worse to think that generally men are unable to appreciate that advertising and the media do not contribute to their perception of women in a positive way.

MIDDLESEX

SOME OF US have had to go through the nightmare of having dirty phone calls. If you look at this cutting you will see *The Sun* are *asking* men to ring the girls up!* That is worse still and encourages not only the worst sex crimes but also dirty phone calls too. Lots of children read these papers. Surely, they must grow up to think that all women are only for one thing.

EAST ANGLIA

WHEN I WAS a child of 7 years, I was put into the care of my mother's friend who had children of her own. This was for a period of around 7 weeks. During that time the husband made my life a nightmare and eventually tried to rape me – it was an horrific experience and I know he abused his children also. I also know he was engrossed in pornographic magazines. I feel very strongly there is a connection between sexual abuse and pornographic material in magazines, videos and the media in general. Some-

* *The Sun*, 16 March 1986.

thing must be done to bring 'respect' back into our society. I fear so much for the future of others as well as ourselves.

KENT

I AM A victim of a sex attack which happened last year. The attacker was fortunately caught straight away and was sentenced at the beginning of March this year. The case was printed in the local papers and almost every time the story was put next to some scantily clad female model which really outraged me. It made a total mockery of what had happened to me.

TOWN WITHHELD

I ALSO BELIEVE that sexual violence and violence towards women generally is fed by pornography, although almost every man I've ever spoken to tries to dissociate male violence from pornography, and pornography from Page 3 journalism.

TOWN WITHHELD

IF PAGE 3 photos don't have any effect on the men who slobber over them, why did some pathetic specimen accost me in a club and bawl 'If you had tits like Sammy Fox, I'd take you home and give you one?' It seems any spotty, pimply youth can make personal cracks about any female who doesn't measure up to his Page 3 expectations. I don't like to have to rely on people for lifts home etc or on taxis. I don't like to be scared to walk down a dark street, or if there are a gang of young blokes on a street corner. I don't see why I should have to take extra care because some sick men have the wrong idea of women. And where do they get the idea of women as just bodies? Page 3. I rest my case.

SUSSEX

IS IT RIGHT that *The Sun* should be able to virtually incite rape by publishing sex surveys which say things like '23-year-old Kate dreams of being tied to a bed and made love to against her will', or 'My sexy dream was being taken by force'. From this men might be stupid enough to think that when a woman says no she means yes.

SCOTLAND

I AM SURE these [pictures] encourage the sexual abuse of women – both verbal and physical – from which I have suffered like so many others. I was indecently assaulted by a stranger when I was 12, on the way home from school (he asked me to direct him to the church and then dragged me in) and I was beaten and raped on an overnight train when I was 22 – when I got home after this I told my boyfriend – instead of sympathy I got rejection as he saw me as being 'shop-soiled'. I have worked in factories where the men all had Page 3 pin-ups above their workbenches, and I dreaded braving the gauntlet of their suggestive remarks when I had to cross the shop floor. Now that I have become flat chested after breastfeeding my 2 children, I am made to feel (*not* by my husband) that I am some kind of unfeminine freak since I do not resemble the stereotyped shape of those misguided model girls.

HERTFORDSHIRE

I HAVE READ the occasional interview given by these models from time to time. From them it seems that they believe they are providing some sort of *service*. In particular a comment made by Samantha Fox which went something like: 'Surely it's better for a guy to look at a picture of me and live out his fantasies that way, than to go out and attack a woman.' (How awfully kind of her! – to put her body at the disposal of men for my sake!) Well, personally I believe that provocative poses in pictures that she (and others of her ilk) appear in, have the *opposite* effect to those she claims they have. *For God's sake, men don't stick them on their walls for a calming effect, quite the opposite!* So if we accept that they have an exciting effect on men (which is only natural – *my argument is, we shouldn't all have to be an unwitting party to it*) – the question is not unreasonable to pose, 'What are they aroused & excited to do?' I am not proposing that every man is a potential rapist, but *if these pictures incite just one man to commit a violent attack on a woman (or women) then that is one man too many.*

TOWN WITHHELD

I CAN THINK of no reason *why* a topless girl should appear in a newspaper, only many reasons why not. Having been a victim of violent sexual behaviour, I feel very strongly that depicting women in provocative poses each day demeans women, suggesting women are playthings for the amusement of men.

SUSSEX

MY FIRST MARRIAGE broke up due to my husband's involvement in these magazines, he was so involved that the time came when smutty mags were not enough and he moved on to pornography and worse, all of which he wanted to try out on me. I knew nothing about his interest until I found some horrific contact magazines offering ridiculous ideas. I know of many marriages where women have returned home unexpected to find their husbands masturbating to these pictures and have been sickened.

DERBY

TWO YEARS AGO, when I was only eighteen, I was sexually assaulted by a man not unfamiliar to me. I knew that the walls of his rented room were covered with topless models from *The Sun* newspaper. He ripped my top off and touched me quite violently. Throughout the assault, which lasted around ten minutes, he repeated over and over what a great Page 3 girl he thought I would make. He seemed to have a fixation about breasts and although he tried, I was able to restrain him from having forced intercourse with me. I have never told anybody about this; I felt cheap being seen as a mindless object and that confiding in anyone would do no good and perhaps make me look bad. However, if what happened to me can help prove that there must be some sort of connection between Page 3 girls and the motivation behind sexual assaults then I feel able to share my unsavoury secret in the hope that something can be done. Because of this event, I am frightened of most men and have come to despise the dumbness and naivity of women like Samantha Fox who have caused so many men to look at women as objects and not individuals with as much, if not more, brain and sensitivity as them.

TOWN WITHHELD

I AM THE victim of 'rape within marriage'. My priest tells me it's all

to do with my husband's feelings of rejection by his mother – by abusing me he's getting at her. Mother and father were extreme prudes and the three boys got their sex education from the back of lavatory walls, girlie magazines and experimenting with equally curious schoolgirls.

My husband is an airline captain and I can only say 'Thank God' his routes do not now include Berlin, where access to blue movies and excessively vile magazines resulted in expectations at home that were beyond me.

Until men learn that delicacy, tenderness and honour are an essential part of their relationships with women, there isn't much hope for us.

SURREY

I HAVE ENCLOSED a copy of the page of *The Sun* concerning myself and my family.* A freelance journalist had sold the 'human interest' story concerning my son, then aged 2, to most of the tabloid newspapers. An article, accompanied by a photo, appeared in most papers. *The Sun* decided to just use my 'mug' shot which had been separated from that of other members of my family and had been 'glamorised'. The 'human interest' story appeared next to the Page 3 woman, and strange as it may seem, I did not make any connection. However, I subsequently received a number of abusive phone calls over a period of days, commencing the same afternoon as the publication. The man pretended to be a reporter and wanted me to go over the facts again, and said he'd seen my picture in *The Sun*. Now, the details involved my 2-year-old son locking us in our bedroom, the lock

* *The Sun*, 27 August 1986. *The Sun* refused to grant us permission to reproduce this story.

jamming and the Fire Brigade getting us out – so there are a
number of turn-ons aren't there? Captivity, bedrooms etc, etc.
However I am sure this occured because my face was juxtaposed
with the Page 3 woman. To me, it felt like we were all 'up for sale'
on that page. I rang the freelance reporter to complain. His reply
was very sympathetic. He had in fact already made it quite clear to
The Sun that he preferred human interest stories *not* to appear on
Page 3. So there's a journalist making the connection too.

TOWN WITHHELD

I FEEL VERY upset by the women who are against any form of
censorship – who seem to think that there is no proof that porn
can lead to violence. If you don't mind I will write from personal
experience. When my stepfather married my mother I was 6 – he
brought with him loads of high class porn. From the age of 6 until
I left home at 19, my home life was surrounded by *Playboy*,
Mayfair, high class paintings, photos and books – he is too much
of a snob to read Maxwell and Murdoch. In most of these images,
violence became more and more popular – and using children. I
was sexually abused by my stepfather, and I am totally sure that
there is a connection. For example, when I was 14 *Playboy* had a
series of articles about child sexuality and the popularising of
child sexual abuse. My stepfather would quote their 'liberal'
attitude. Although there may not be any 'real' proof that porn
leads to violence – all I say is, I remember my stepfather showing
me porn, quoting porn before or during abusing me. I know porn
leads to violence. But, of course, there is no proof because the
'victims' are women, and they have been silenced. Most women
who have been through sexual violence are forced to feel guilty. I
just want to stop having to defend myself from not liking porn.
The porn industry should be forced to defend itself from the
crime of gross violence to women. But that seems to be a pipe
dream.

CHESHIRE

THE STAR CHOSE to go into great detail regarding the rape of a 15-
year-old schoolgirl. To me the report read more like pornography
than journalism – describing what the rapist said to the girl, how he

'fondled' and 'stroked' her. Then directly opposite this report there are photos of another schoolgirl in full school uniform and then the same girl topless. I think that putting these two items side by side together like that is extremely provocative, arousing and indeed confusing. It comes across as though schoolgirls just love to be fondled and stroked, look, here is a real schoolgirl showing her breasts, that alongside the sexually stimulating account of the poor rape victim's ordeal amounts virtually to provocation to rape . . .

I was raped several years ago and am as convinced now as I was then that this type of newspaper reporting contributes to the attitudes of men towards women and this in turn causes and encourages rape.

LONDON

AN EVEN MORE worrying aspect of this is the apparent sexual-isation of children in newspapers: recent publicity given to the fact that Bill Wyman of the Rolling Stones had a 13-year-old lover; numerous articles about the 'affectionately titled' Wild Child Emma Ridley, who at 15 has a 30-year-old husband; most alarming of all, in Friday's edition of *Today* was a 2 page article about the latest sex symbol – age 12!* When is all this going to stop? I am convinced that there is a direct link between the sexualisation of children and child sex crimes. How can news-papers justify waxing indignant about a child rapist on Page 1, and then show a half-naked 15 year old on Page 3? If you get a chance, please mention the alarming increase in the number of young girls, some almost pre-pubescent, being presented to the public in a sexual way.

CHESTER

I CAN ONLY say I felt a sudden release from the pressure I had been under when I saw that other women feel as I do, and the feelings I have been fighting to understand about Page 3 girls has finally

* *Today*, 29 January 1988. This was a story about 12-year-old Milla Jovovich who, the paper said, had 'the face of a seductress, the body of a nymphet and the calculating business mind of a woman twice her age'.

been put into print. I want to tell you that your action means more than anything to me. I want to make those who would criticise you realise what is happening before they close their minds to what is a horrific and growing problem in disguise of sexiness and fun.

I am 18, and a few months ago I was raped. My attacker spoke to me during the rape and all he could say was how like a Page 3 girl I was and how my bust would look great in the paper for all the men to see. So, for me to hear someone like yourself say there is a connection between the two is just a huge relief and it gives me hope I did not have before. I want the people who think the two things are unrelated to realise that these 'innocent naughties' are creating danger and fear, apart from degrading women to a sickeningly low level. Apart from my own experience of rape and the humiliation and degradation of being seen as a sex toy and used as one, I can say I felt as much against Page 3 and other forms of exploitation before as I did after my experience.

TOWN WITHHELD

AT THE AGE of 10, almost 11, I was taunted and molested by a man of about 60, some of the things he said and did are in my mind forever and the assaults to my body are forgotten in so much as the love and support of a terrific husband puts them into the perspective they deserve. The most frightening thing this man did was to make me look at all these 'pictures' of ladies' naked forms and poses – today's soft porn and his insistence that what he was doing to me then was because one day I would 'look' like those pictures and when 'men' did those things to me I'd remember. HOW TRUE.

ESSEX

WHEN I READ about the girl who was raped 'because she looked like a Page 3 girl called Jackie', I was hurt for her, but also relieved, because I am sure I only escaped rape by sheer luck. I had been to Manchester and coming back the man who sat next to me straightaway opened his newspaper to look at Page 3. This embarrassed me, but I pretended not to notice, but he kept looking first at the picture, then at me and kept looking me over and staring at my bust. To make it worse, the girl in the picture had long blonde hair, like me, and did look similar. I thought, 'My God. He's thinking he's looking at me nude'. I gave him a look and turned the other way, but could still feel his eyes on me. It was awful and I actually felt that I was sat there naked. It was a dreadful journey. When I got up the man said 'It could almost be you, this, darlin''. I thought maybe it was coincidence but no he was following me, because when I got up to leave the bus so did he. I decided to complain to the bus driver, but when the man said 'I'm not following her but I keep looking at her because she looks like her' (with this he turned to the nude). I was really taken aback with what the driver said, 'she does doesn't she, I wouldn't mind her'. I felt sick. I had asked another man for help and I got the same male abuse. I stormed off the bus as they were laughing. I tried to run but my legs wouldn't seem to let me. I saw an open door and just ran straight in. I was petrified. I explained to the people at the house that this man had followed me. The husband went out but he had gone. The police said they could do nothing. I am now afraid to go out alone, even during the day. I distrust men in general now. Ask the male MP how he would feel if his wife, girlfriend or daughter was raped? Page 3 is not 'a bit of fun' as they say. They should be women, then they would know how we feel.

TOWN WITHHELD

WHAT I OBJECT to most strongly is the way in which these pin-ups portray females as passive, willing, totally available sex objects for men's use and amusement. Whether it be for sexual use or as a punchbag for men to vent their anger and violence on. So many women (and children) are living in fear today without bullying sadistic husbands and fathers. I think that the newspapers who have for the last 15 or so years flooded people's minds with images of females in a sexual context only, must take a large portion of blame for the way in which society treats its females today. It is time for every decent minded woman and man to let their voice be heard, and to try and make our country a safer place for women everywhere.

If one woman or child is saved the terrible ordeal of being assaulted, raped or worse, by the banning of pin-ups then it will be worth it. It will take a long time, but people have got to be re-educated to see females as human beings with feelings and basic rights, and not as presented by the gutter press, as a joke, and a dirty joke at that.

SUNDERLAND

I FIND THE judge's remarks offensive to an extraordinary degree.* As a widow I have brought up three children. I have worked hard to see that they should be well educated and I feel that all women and particularly young women should be judged and respected for what they are – their minds, souls, characters and ability to do their jobs – not their bodies. I do not think this judge realises that until men see women in a proper way, we shall continue to have women raped, assaulted, abused and discriminated against. People who hold public office and make public announcements should understand that with privilege goes responsibility. Men like him have a duty to set a proper example to other men. If this article is true I would ask you to bring it before the Lord Chancellor.

TOWN WITHHELD

IT WILL BE impossible to reduce the crime of rape until men adopt some collective responsibility.

LONDON

* This was a piece about how the notorious Judge Pickles had claimed 'I Like Page 3 Girls', *Today*, 22 April 1989.

If You Don't Like it, You Don't Have to Buy it

Do women have a choice?

One of the arguments used in the pornography debate is that if people don't like it they are free not to buy it, the implication being that they are therefore free from its effects. This is a highly simplistic argument. Page 3 cannot be cordoned off like a nasty accident. Its effects are all-pervasive. It is not just a harmless pastime for the few who indulge. Women may exercise their freedom to choose not to buy, read or model in these papers, but they have to live in a society with those who do. Women have very little or no control over the material that helps define men's perception of them. Nor do they have control over the timing and location of its exposure.

The issue of the public display of pornography in newspapers has become very confused. Newsagents display pornography under sections entitled General Interest or Leisure. Because of their refusal to call pornography by its name, those who object – rather than those who indulge – are alienated. Women have general interests too and the placing of porn in these sections makes them feel unwelcome – especially if someone is thumbing through top shelf titles at eye level.

Page 3 porn is available on the bottom shelf. The explicit front pages of *The Sunday Sport* are still displayed next to the comics despite a Press Council judgement that it should be stocked alongside pornography.* Other 'general' magazines like *Video World* contain more pornographic material and all these titles are within easy reach. The growth in newspaper advertisements for sex-industry related goods, videos, chatlines etc has further blurred the distinction between newspapers and magazines which are recognised as pornographic.

While porn has always been available, it is Page 3 that has made it acceptable and its continual presence tolerated. It has

* A Press Council adjudication, 5 November 1989.

engendered attitudes in a way that no other 'nudge-nudge' treatment has. *Carry On* films, 'saucy' postcards etc were understood to be comical farce. There is nothing farcical about this systematic harassment. The objectification of the female body is now considered justifiable light entertainment; its effects are far from light and women have little respite from them. Pornography is everywhere – in the newspapers, on the tube, at station kiosks, in the workplace, in advertising. It has become an acceptable part of our culture.

I DON'T WANT to be embarrassed when one of the daily papers is brought into my home, for it's my home and I shouldn't need to be embarrassed. I am the only girl in the house. I live with my two brothers and my father and it can be very embarrassing. So now you know that you have my full support to pass the bill. GOOD LUCK. Yours hopefully . . .

CAMBRIDGESHIRE

IN SOME WAYS, Page 3 (or whatever page) does more harm than 'porn' books because they are *pushed* at us *every* single day of *every* week; they also inflict views on our children – even young children. I do not have the papers myself, but a lot of women have no choice, as that is what the husbands insist as mine did once. I also agree with you about the way women are exploited sexually for purposes of advertising etc – we are threatened as one reader put it from every angle – trains, buses etc. . . .

TOWN WITHHELD

CONSTANT DEPICTION OF nude women in attitudes of coy submission and availability must only help to confirm, however unconsciously in the minds of some men, their right to exploit and depersonalise women. Society does on the one hand indignantly condemn the degradation of women and yet on the other, openly condones it.

HAMPSHIRE

IN MY LIBRARY (near school) boys come in sniggering at *The Daily Mirror* Page 3 during their lunchtimes. I don't have to buy/read them but worry about the effects on boys' attitudes to women and possibly their anger/frustrations vented on women because we don't excite or come 'down' to their expectations of us, and their perpetual state of arousal and what to do with it.

I consider these papers and the girls in them irresponsible.

OXFORD

I HAD LOWERED my eyes in embarrassment from a vulgar offering waving before me in the bus and, incidentally tried to locate a *Vogue* magazine on the top shelf in W.H. Smiths without having to pore over a clutch of vulvas and breasts invitingly exposed alongside, *yet again* recently, when I just cracked.

LANCASHIRE

NOT LONG AGO I was standing in the local branch of W.H. Smiths. As I scanned the magazine shelves my eyes fell on the open pages of a 'soft porn' magazine held by a man standing next to me. I am not a 'prude' but, and I have seen these magazines before, it suddenly hit me how disgusting the whole thing is. I left the shop nearly in tears. Why, when all I want to do is buy a magazine, should it be possible for a man next to me to openly display a double-page spread of a female in a sexual pose. I felt very scared and humiliated. This is in the middle of the afternoon in a High Street shop. Why is it that these publications are not sealed and more discreetly covered?

It may be a human right that a man or woman is free to buy such magazines, but I think it is a more important human right that myself and my children can enter a newsagent and not be subjected to such images. Big deal that they are displayed on the top shelf – when an adult is making his selection it happens to be at the eye level of children that the pages are opened.

I am fed up with having to pretend not to see displays of sex magazines and titillating pictures of women in newspapers, all of which show only deep contempt for women.

TOWN WITHHELD

I RECENTLY FELT obliged to leave our local sports club because the steward thought that Samantha Fox in her 'natural glory' was a suitable calendar for the next twelve months. He removed it at my husband's request but I feel very angry that he commented on not being able to understand why it upset me. It seems women are expected to take no offence or if they do to keep their opinions to themselves. There will always be macho morons who talk about freedom of choice. What about our freedom to open a daily paper or walk into a pub without being confronted by this rubbish?

I have heard men say that it is just a bit of fun. I wonder how funny they would find it if their womenfolk opened the paper and leered at Page 3 pictures of nude men or went into their local and passed remarks about the fully exposed pictures of the 'Man of the Month' calendar. They'd choke on their beer. Men wouldn't stand for their sex being demeaned. Why should we?

I feel that if the House of Commons were made up largely of women the problem would have been dealt with and the horrific flood of sexual attacks on women stemmed. It is largely a women's problem. We make up half the population yet the politicians treat us with such derision on this issue. It is the fear of ridicule which keeps a lot of women silent.

TOWN WITHHELD

I DO NOT buy the papers concerned, but if I happen to see one of these pictures I feel personally insulted – and devalued as a woman. The sight of young boys sniggering over them and defacing them fills me with despair as does the treatment of women on television.

A young girl I spoke to recently said she didn't watch television anymore because it was all about *hurting* women, and she was fearful enough as it was.

Can it be right for half the population to spend their lives in fear and apprehension of the other half?

TOWN WITHHELD

Dressing to Please

Problems with Self-Image

The constant exposure to images of physical female perfection creates a standard by which all women are judged. We are all more familiar with a diversity of perfect images than with individual bodies – flawed or otherwise. The existence of a standard means that a woman must either conform to a male defined stereotype – cute, thin, leggy, blonde, busty – or be dismissed as a deviant from this artificial norm.

This standard is false and synthetic. It is man-made. Nevertheless it is the standard by which all women are judged. It is a man's world and, in judging women, that world prioritises a woman's looks above all else.

Failure to live up to this standard is a device often used to silence women. Nowhere can this be seen more clearly than the way in which the tabloids treated Clare Short at the time of the Bill. They implied that because she didn't fit the Page 3 stereotype, her objections stemmed from jealousy. *The Star* called her 'notably unsexy', *The Sun* called her 'Ms Misery'. The accompanying pictures of Clare Short showed her in as unflattering a light as possible. Personal appearance was a notable weapon in the tabloids' dismissal of her viewpoint.

Women know how necessary it is for them to look good to be noticed and in order to have a voice. It takes time to make yourself presentable – and we are not just talking about a wash and brush-up – we are talking about creating an image that will conform and reinforce male notions of what a woman is.

Given this fact, women are presented with a difficult choice – to ignore the demands upon her for a so-called pleasing appearance and risk being socially marginalised or conform to the pressures and risk being stereotyped as shallow, and accused of obsessive concern for her looks ('typical woman'). Her vanity is a standard joke, but concern with her appearance is in fact a basic requirement for a woman to be accepted.

This creates blurred distinctions whereby it is difficult for women to know whether she is doing things for herself or to please men, since in pleasing men an individual improves her chances in a man's world as far as social status is concerned. It is impossible to exist without some form of interaction so at some level every woman has to compromise. This ambiguity can account for the almost apologetic tone in some of the following letters. Women can feel guilty about succumbing to a male ideal – dying their hair, shaving their legs and armpits, dieting, wearing make-up – but are fearful of the personal consequences if they don't concede in terms of their employment prospects, relationships with men and so on.

Beauty is a cultural perception, and in this white-dominated society, the Page 3 notion of womanhood is a very Anglo-Saxon one. She is very often blonde, always pretty, very young and rarely black. How often are women of a different ethnicity 'used' on Page 3? Real women have no place there. It is not just that women choose – or choose not – to be a Page 3 clone but that by its very structure, it excludes a vast number of women because they never will fit the bill. And when black women do appear on Page 3 they are usually referred to as 'dusky beauty'. They are racistly stereotyped, as athletic, animalistic and closer to nature. The notion of black and Asian women as exotic increases their alienation from a society that already denies them the little voice their sisters have.

When a naked woman looks at her body, she knows how it compares with the standard, where it falls short and where it surpasses. The woman who can resist a selfconscious appraisal of her own body is a very strong woman indeed. For some women, the self-conscious 'upgrading' mentality that society encourages them to develop can lead to eating disorders such as anorexia nervosa and bulimia as symptomatic of an obsessive desire to control their bodies.* These disorders often occur in women who are constantly exposed from an early age to the unrealistic standard required of them, or to perceptions of female sexuality that they find disturbing.

* Anorexia nervosa and bulimia are separate but related eating disorders. Simplistically, anorexia is characterised by fasting and bulimia by binging and purging. The causes of both disorders are many and complex, but both are most common in adolescent girls and women.

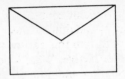

WE MUST RECLAIM our bodies. I don't want to have to go on feeling sick and powerless every time I enter W.H. Smiths.

TOWN WITHHELD

I AGREE WHOLEHEARTEDLY with your proposals. I'm sick and tired of hearing about the body beautiful. Particularly as I have a physically handicapped daughter. She is 23 and thankfully unaffected by the media's hype on what the perfect female should be like. It's time we valued women for the good they do, not for how good they look. Edwina Currie is quoted as saying her husband 'would prefer her to look like Samantha Fox'. How degrading for her. Any self respecting woman would tell him to pack his bags. Pronto.

GLOUCESTERSHIRE

WE ARE SICK to our stomachs (literally) that women are treated in such a degrading and objective manner. We know we are worth more. We are also working and striving for respect for women. One New Zealand paper cancelled Page 3 girls in 1984. Another publishes token Page 2 boys but the pictures are smaller and have more integrity. We also battle to have all Page 3s banned.

CHRISTCHURCH (NZ), ANOREXIA & BULIMIA GROUP

I LIKE TO look good, too. But I like to look good for ME. For my own satisfaction. I don't need a man's approval to feel satisfied with myself. And if I do look good that certainly doesn't give any man the right to take me by force, or to disregard what I say to him.

Whatever we wear, wherever we go,
Yes means Yes. And No means No.

Why is that such a difficult concept for a man? Portrayals of women as cute and pretty and thin can mean that the vast majority of women who do not fit into this narrow stereotype feel guilty, wrong-shaped and unattractive. What kind of person we are in our attitudes, co-operation and support of others is far more important than our visual appearance.

TOWN WITHHELD

AS A TEENAGER I found these pictures very upsetting, not really knowing why. Fellow girl-friends felt the same. I tried to rationalise it, but why should we have to endure this humiliation?

TOWN WITHHELD

I THINK THAT Page 3 does more harm than pornographic books, because they are easier to come by and affect children as well as adults. Some male MPs have been quoted as saying that women who complain are flatchested prudes 'who would never take their children to art museums'. This is sheer nonsense. I am young and like to look nice and I am certainly not flatchested. Also, I like to take my children to art museums. I think men . . . use a lot of Page 3 remarks to women. Because I have a big bust a lot of remarks from men are awful and at one stage I got so embarassed that I refused to take my coat off when I went out. I don't wear low cut, tight dresses or anything like that. I am really fed up of it.

TOWN WITHHELD

PAGE 3 GIRLS send out one message to people, mainly women, and that message is: women, your man will not lust or love you if you are not pretty, have big boobs and blonde hair. You have to have curvy figures and say silly things and act dumb. If you don't fit into this Page 3 mould, then you are worthless, ugly and no man will give you a glance. I am not a raving feminist, I do have feminist views and why not, why should women be pulled down and degraded. I cannot escape from the fact that this is what men want. I still feel fat, ugly and unwanted as my boyfriend secretly eyes up Page 3 as if to say 'This is my kind of dream girl, not you'. I am forever fighting to keep slim (almost anorexic at one stage), dye my hair blonde and dress up. It makes me sick that these pin-ups are ogled over by grown men with families, maybe they are upholding their male image, but us women need to campaign to show our anger. I feel sorry for these pin-up girls really – men don't see them as they really are, maybe clever, maybe not. They do have to earn a living but why degrade themselves? and us?

NOTTINGHAMSHIRE

IT MAKES ME SO angry to see women portrayed in this way that I can usually only blurt out a furious objection. But I have realised recently that it has a much more profound effect upon me. My perception of myself, especially certain parts of myself which I need not make explicit, have, I believe, been affected by these pictures. A woman's breasts are beautiful but for me their beauty has been polluted by the way they are used to sell newspapers – many other products use the female form to promote sales. How would men feel about their penises if they saw them portrayed daily in a provocative scantily clad fashion in order to sell a product.

Women will always be vulnerable as long as they are portrayed as passive, available, fragmented and without needs and emotions of their own.

TOWN WITHHELD

PAGE 3 WOMEN are there for those who can only dream – 'If only my wife had knockers like that, if only'. An MP said that the Page 3 women were good for the relief of sexual tensions. Surely the reverse is true? They only perpetuate the myth and give rise to frustration which would not be there if men could only be satisfied with what they have.

SOUTH YORKSHIRE

MY EXPERIENCE IS that the naked human person is at his most vulnerable and defenceless. People say if you are frightened of someone, imagine what he is like without his clothes on. Even a baby looks more helpless naked. Whether in fact these pictures are strictly pornographic is not relevant. It is that women should not be portrayed as more defenceless than we need to be, giving the impression we are a pushover. Why I always wonder do men class pictures of naked men as obscene but not women? Because it would destroy the macho image?

TOWN WITHHELD

IT MAY BE of interest to you to hear that through our own experience I am convinced that there are other aspects to this – not just the ones of corruption and depravity. For instance, nobody seems to know why the incidence of illnesses such as anorexia nervosa are becoming so widespread – they only know that it is almost impossible to cure them. Our own daughter suffered from this illness for eight years, and it lead ultimately to drug addiction and misery. She had been terribly shocked at the age of about 12 or 13, on her way home from school, seeing a grey haired man sitting in his parked car at the kerbside looking at magazine pictures of nude girls. She ran home and locked her door – and later explained to me what had upset her. I feel so sad now, that something so apparently trivial should have had such a profound effect on a sensitive child at a sensitive age. There may be countless others who have been similarly disturbed while not necessarily depraved. This was one of several incidents which led to her becoming anorexic at 14½ – and losing the rest of her childhood. Please persevere.

EDINBURGH

I AM MIDDLE aged, short and fat – pornography apparently has nothing to do with me. Yet when I walk past a group of young people, especially young men (or for that matter males of any age) I am almost invariably subjected to abuse. Sometimes this is overt, offensive remarks shouted at me, or catcalls, most times it is covert, whispering and sniggering. When I requested, very politely, a young man to reduce the volume on his radio he and all his mates subjected me to considerable verbal abuse on account of my fatness.

The reason grown men feel able – even entitled – to make such derogatory remarks is because of pornography. I don't mean the 'sex shop' stuff only, but the Page 3 and advertisement variety of pornography too. I won't call it 'soft porn' since there is nothing soft about any form of violence and this *is* violence. The media portray an image of women: they treat the female body as common property, so 'entitling' others to make remarks about me, they portray only one (rare) type of female body, creating and fostering the notion that this is how a woman ought to look, legitimating and encouraging the opinion that I am a deviant and not entitled to respect.

WEST YORKSHIRE

MANY WOMEN I know object to Page 3 girls and the representation of women in the media on the grounds that it does encourage sexual and violent crimes against women, but also because it reinforces the ideology of women as objects of pleasure for men, whose identity is then determined by their physical attributes and defined by their relationships to men. Moreover it operates as a 'divide and rule' tactic amongst women, with women who are not sexy, sultry playmates being made to feel envious of those who are, and boring spoilsports if they say anything against this blatant titillation.

TOWN WITHHELD

PORNOGRAPHY IS A powerful weapon used to demoralise women. By reducing them to mere sex objects they pose no threat intellectually, or so it is hoped by men who portray women in this way. To some extent I think they have been successful unfortunately, because the beautiful women who appear in the media are the yardsticks that men use to measure other women by. Good looks and sensual figures gain credibility and are still rewarded with good parts in films, the media in general, and good jobs etc. These natural, and in some cases not so natural, attributes take precedence over skills. No-one likes to feel or be compared – it makes them feel vulnerable. The sensitivities of men are protected. They are not to be seen in titillating poses on Page 3, nor are they seen posing scantily clad on top of motor cars, yet women buy cars. How often do we see male actors languishing in bed with their genitals in full view? Who'd want to? you may well say, and I would agree. But the fact is men's feelings are protected, they are not made to feel compared and maybe wanting . . . because they are brothers under the skin they protect themselves and other men from scrutiny.

Pornography is divisive where women are concerned, because a young woman with a good figure and fresh looks will not react in perhaps the same way as a middle-aged mother of three would react to a nude scene where some young nubile woman is making love on the screen. A young woman may feel more secure about her face and figure and therefore less threatened than an older woman who would feel more threatened and intimidated because of the excessive amount of attention given by the media to the young and beautiful.

The labelling of women who complain about pornography as jealous prudes has proved to be a very effective way of silencing opposition to it. Even if this is the case women have a right to their thoughts and feelings. Their right is legitimate.

TOWN WITHHELD

THE BODY OF an attractive young woman (or man) is a delight to see and I have no time for excessive prudery nor do I have any objection to topless bathing or nudist camps. Nevertheless I am concerned about these pictures because of their effect on both young men and women.

Even in well balanced and honourable men the treatment of women in pin-ups can lead them to a superficial view of their fellow citizens. For the young, the impressionable, and those whose upbringing has not taught them respect for women, the consequences could be disastrous leading to them, at best, failing to form whole relationships and at worst making them believe that sexual assault is acceptable and even expected.

For women, I feel they encourage a lack of self respect and confidence. Young girls see them as an image and if they themselves do not 'measure up' it can cause them to suffer greatly. Older women who like me have succumbed through childbirth away from neat, flawless figures to bags and stretch-marks may see themselves finished as women and no longer possessing value, when in fact their maturity, experience and understanding make them better friends, better partners and better citizens.

MANCHESTER

RECENTLY A FRIEND of mine has undergone a biopsy for a mastectomy and having pictures of women's breasts constantly on public display adds to a deeply felt pain. Another colleague recently attending her GP for back pain was told to improve her posture and stick her chest out like a Page 3 girl. The GP incidentally was male. Tonight on BBC2 is a programme about Page 3 in which a young 15-year-old is hopeful.* Need I say more? This insidious portrayal of the female image in this way is extremely dangerous and damaging to any attempt for women to operate on an equal social standing to men. I and many other women will not tolerate these irresponsible views being made by Members of Parliament, and will support you and other women in a campaign that will ban sexism in the gutter press, adverts etc.

TOWN WITHHELD

I DO FEEL that there is a connection between these pictures and the increase in rapes. But what is also alarming is that it misleads many insecure girls and women to believe that it is only by being sexually provocative that they can ever be objects of love and affection or through only seeing their bodies as worthwhile, they undervalue themselves.

The press here made a great emphasis on how these girls say that they do not feel exploited and a naked body is a beautiful thing. So it is but they will only see the true extent to which they have been exploited when this year's bodies and faces of the moment are cast aside for next years. It would be interesting to try and follow up the histories of the girls who appeared in *The Sun* several years ago. Where are they now? Remember Marilyn Monroe. God help Samantha Fox in ten or fifteen years time when she has to come to terms with the signs of aging. As a teacher I find that it is the most uncared for girls who become sexually

* *40 Minutes*, BBC2, 27 May 1986.

provocative and easy prey for men who will just use them. For many girls sexual encounters are a search for love. These models are sending them down the wrong road and a dangerous one at that. For boys and men the photos trivialise women and present them as merely objects for self-gratification.

LONDON

HOW I FEEL is that breasts shown in papers in the seductive way that they are can become very degrading towards women who earn a living by working and doing ordinary jobs every day. I feel a difference between exposure in newspapers and magazines and that of a mother breastfeeding, for example.

I am 23 years of age. I have a boyfriend of 4 years and to be totally honest with you we row constantly every day over Page 3 girls. My family can't understand me. My boyfriend has tried to help me so much by explaining to me that him looking at a topless picture in *The Sun* means absolutely nothing to him. But still I fret and feel so angry about those pictures. Surely a newspaper is to provide news not 'nudes'. Although I don't buy any paper I know would contain topless pictures I know my boyfriend will at sometime during the day look at *The Sun*, seeing as he works on a building site.

I have heard men talking and wolf-whistling at women, and the reason is because we are looked upon as sex symbols. I also feel that the increase in child abuse, rape etc has happened because there is too much exposure of female bodies. I would have a better relationship, I would feel relaxed if the situation were improved. In fact at times I get so worked up when discussing this with my boyfriend and trying to make him see why I won't let him touch me, look at me, talk to me – because it actually affects me in this way when he looks in *The Sun* . . .

GLOUCESTERSHIRE

Whose Breasts are they Anyway?

The Breastfeeding Dilemma

The constant media exposure of breasts, in ways designed to titillate and arouse men, suggests that men have more claim on them than women. Newspapers, advertisers, men, babies – make multiple claims on them and society forgets whose breasts they really are. There is no other part of the body – male or female – that is hived off from the whole and used as a commodity in its own right. Not even the penis, which is glorified more in innuendo than in familiarity, and in any case is meant to represent something about the virility and character of the male. Objectification of the breast denies true ownership and true purpose. A woman is more than the sum of her parts but in a society which places so much emphasis on individual features, she is treated as not even equal to them.

With so many images of naked breasts on display, so few of them positive, how is a woman to feel about her own breasts? The images surrounding her are almost exclusively sexual and very often cheap. Women are ill at ease with this part of their body. They worry about its adequacy for their husbands, lovers, babies. Faced daily with images of so-called perfection women, when looking at their own bodies, see only their shortcomings. It is hardly surprising many feel ambivalent towards them.

Breasts *are* sexual but this is only one small part of a woman's sexual expression. Sexuality comes from within. Try and over-signify a man's genitalia and he will tell you 'it's not the size of your wand but the magic you weave with it'.

In wearing low cut or skimpy clothing – because it's hot, because she feels like it – a woman is accused of being provocative. She is required to respect the definition of that part of her body as 'purely sexual' but not contest in any way society's authority to expose this sexuality when and where it sees fit. We have become unable to see a naked breast without associating it with sexy romps and Page 3 'fun'.

Breastfeeding is a public assertion by a woman of her rights over her own body, the timing and nature of its exposure. This is a natural and important act but often causes great consternation. Breastfeeding mothers are often asked to leave restaurants or to go in to discreet places so as not to offend people.* It is ironic that the sexual whimsy of a tabloid reading male is publicly accommodated in a way that the biological needs of a mother and baby are not. People are confused by the public display of a breast in circumstances that are clearly not sexual. Very often, it is other women who feel uncomfortable with public breastfeeding – understandably so given that the breast is constantly displayed as something to lust or laugh over. Women feel exposed. This is because they have come to associate this part of their body with something distasteful to them. These letters discuss the hypocritical embarrassment of a society when faced with real breasts.

I FEEL THAT ordinary men who regularly see pornography become desensitised and increasingly aggressive towards women. This leads to more violent relationships and more incidental harassment. I think the effects of pornography are more widespread than first appears. As a health visitor, I encourage breastfeeding but am aware of the unnatural and unhealthy attitude women have towards their own breasts. They are almost taboo for their owners. It's as if they are not a part of the woman's self. They are the property of the man in the relationship. I feel this is in part responsible for the low take-up of breastfeeding in less educated women.

LANCASHIRE

I BELIEVE THAT the adverse reaction of men to breastfeeding in

* In a survey conducted by The National Childbirth Trust in 1989, the facilities that 70% of restaurants said they provided for breastfeeding mothers were actually toilets.

public has a lot to do with our present culture that displays women's bodies as fulfilling male sexual needs only.

LONDON

I HAVE JUST started training as a breastfeeding counsellor with the National Childbirth Trust. I believe that to breastfeed a child is to give it the best possible start in life – nutritionally, emotionally and developmentally. So many babies are being denied this gift because of these Page 3 pictures. It is hardly surprising that so many women are put off breastfeeding by the images portrayed leading women to believe that their bodies are solely for the purpose of attracting men. No wonder they feel selfconscious about the idea of breastfeeding, let alone overwhelmed by the practicalities of it.

TOWN WITHHELD

HOW MANY COMPLAINTS would there be if women breastfed their young openly on buses, trains, in pubs, offices, on the street etc? Yet no-one objects to naked women in newspapers, read and displayed in all these places.

LIVERPOOL

THIS MATTER WAS highlighted for me because I had just returned from the doctor's with my baby. The person sitting next to me was reading *The Sun*, and these girls were openly displayed, yet it occurred to me that if I were to start breastfeeding my baby, there would be more than a few raised eyebrows. I really think society has gone mad, and I was very disappointed to hear the jeering of the male MPs when you were speaking in Parliament yesterday.

WATFORD

THERE IS A great deal of hypocrisy in our society when it comes to the baring of women's breasts in public. Page 3 displays seem to be perfectly acceptable yet breastfeeding mothers are not. When I breastfeed my 4-month-old son, I ensure that it is done as discreetly as possible. I do not 'bare all' to the world. Yet in one large department store, my friend and I were asked to stop as it 'wasn't very nice for the other customers'. In all fairness, the staff did provide us with a room in which we could eat and feed our babies but it didn't stop us feeling like social outcasts.

LANCASHIRE

I FEEL THERE is surely something sick in a society that glorifies (and pays extraordinary amounts for) exposed breasts and yet provides me with a cubicle in a toilet to feed my baby in.

SUSSEX

BREASTS ARE SUCH lovely things – so useful for feeding babies and such a cosy place for tired children or overworked husbands to lay their heads and to see breasts turned into objects of impersonal lust is very upsetting to any woman. However, we are not our breasts; our breasts are not the whole of us; they are a small part of our physical and emotional make-up – not mere unconnected bits of flesh.

EAST YORKSHIRE

Your Freedom to Swing Your Arm Ends Where my Nose Begins

The Censorship Debate

This is the issue on which much pornography debate founders and is the major axis for many of the political discussions about Page 3 for feminists, trade unions, pornographers etc. This obsession with censorship has been allowed to overshadow all other considerations – even that of violence against women. The sanctity of its position has become more important to almost everyone – even the traditionally sympathetic Left – than the basic rights of women to live free from fear.

Censorship is a dirty word and one that is thrown in to this debate in an attempt to stifle it. Most people understand the word censorship to mean banning things – but some things *should* be banned and many already are. The Race Relations Act 1976 recognises the necessity of banning material which can incite violence or hatred. People are banned from killing one another, torturing one another, lying about one another in print – all these things are in some way a form of censorship. People recognise that this state intervention is essential in a civilised society. Censorship is only dangerous when it is used by the state or those with excessive power to prevent that power being challenged or to repress any alternative expression that is threatening to them.

Page 3 itself is censorship. Page 3 intimidates, silences and lies about women. Can it be wrong to stop these images when so many feel they are harmed by them? Can it be censorship to remove this intimidation? Can it truly be censorship to give a voice to those who are usually silent? Censorship is about definitions of reality and the power of any one single group to make these definitions. Those without power cannot even hope to impose censorship on anyone. All they can hope to do is to redress the imbalance of power in their own favour.

There is no doubt that a ban on Page 3 would restrict some men's freedoms but the freedoms women would gain far outweigh that sacrifice. The freedom to see porn on a daily basis must be set against the freedom from fear and alienation. His luxuries hinder her survival.

Civil libertarians claim that if current censorship laws were amended, reactionary groups would use them to ban sexually educational material, gay and lesbian erotica and erotic literature. In the light of Clause 28 this is a very real fear but if we are clear about our terms, there need not be any confusion. Robert Adley tried to suggest that Page 3 and works of art were, broadly speaking, the same thing. The women who wrote to Clare Short clearly felt there was a great difference. Sexually explicit material is not necessarily pornography and pornography need not be sexually explicit – as the saccharine Page 3 demonstrates. Greater clarification and classification would benefit everybody.

Support for Clare Short's Bill was wide-ranging. Feminists and church groups, Conservatives and Socialists found themselves strangely aligned on the issue of pornography. For whatever reason, many people feel that pornography is to the detriment of society. On this point, and this point alone, they agree. The fact that so many diverse groups are looking to some form of censorship as a solution indicates the strength of concern.

Those worried about further empowering the state are being defeatist. Women would like to reclaim the legislative bodies of state and make them work as they were intended. Women want representation; why should we relinquish Government as our recourse to this end? Parliament is there for us to act for us. In the debate about freedoms, why is the freedom to offend more respected than the freedom to object? The nature and availability of this material is seriously affecting the quality of our lives. Where pornography is concerned, the censorship debate is a luxury that many women feel they can no longer afford.

NORMALLY, I AM opposed to censorship and certainly feel uncomfortable at the thought of aligning with the Whitehouse contingent, but on this issue I feel a move has to be made for the sake of women's dignity. Tabloid nudity and its ilk is utterly demeaning to women, emphasising literally day in, day out to men that they don't need to take women seriously; that women – all women – are there for them to pore over, judge and use at will. Women should not be put off their opposition to this image by the old accusations of 'prudishness' and 'narrowmindedness'.

The appalling behaviour of your male colleagues in the House –our supposedly responsible representatives – only goes to prove how total is society's general disrespect for women and also how this disrespect is allied to a juvenile fear of women in many men; there was something desperate in the catcalls . . .

TOWN WITHHELD

I AM QUITE convinced that Page 3 contributes to a general lowering of respect for all women, and there must be a high probability of this diminished respect being linked to the increased sexual attacks on women of all ages. Goebbels used pornographic images of Jews to reduce public respect for them and so make it easier to induce the German public to accept the hideous treatment of Jews in Nazi Germany, and his propaganda was highly effective as we all know. I am not suggesting there is a deliberate campaign to eliminate women in this country but I am sure that pornography and Page 3 nudes have a disastrous effect on men's attitudes towards women.

I have found that your parliamentary campaign is being much discussed among women – everyone that I know has mentioned it at some time in the last few weeks – and I have yet to hear a single woman speak against you. You have absolutely touched a raw nerve amongst women throughout the country.

SUSSEX

I HAVE LOST count of the number of arguments I have had with civil libertarians (mostly male) who deride all suggestions about stopping pornography because it would infringe freedom of speech and involve censorship. These are always seen as the master values – and yet it is now accepted that anti-racism can be more important than freedom of speech, so why not stopping violence against women?

BRISTOL

I FIND IT discomforting that I may be dealing, in everyday life, with men whose attitude to women is formed by women's easy availability in a passive and purely sexual role on the pages of newspapers and magazines. As for the 'logical' arguments that censorship will inevitably lead to the banning of Shakespeare etc, common sense tells us the difference between art and exploitation. There will be a grey area but perhaps it is time to change our priorities from erring in favour of *laissez faire* to erring on the side of respect for individuals and protection of women and children from exploitation and criminality.

TOWN WITHHELD

THERE ARE ENOUGH sick men, unfortunately, who read these type of newspapers daily, who have come to the conclusion from this daily ugly perpetuation of young girls' bodies, that these girls are to be had sexually by men, whatever the cost, be it rape, murder, or whatever. The comment from several people about what the difference is between paintings of nude women in museums and the Page 3 photos in newspapers is preposterous. There is an incredible difference between art and pornography and I feel very sorry for anyone who does not know the difference. Art lifts up the spirit of humanity and is a mirror on the beauty, perplexity of the individual person. If it's good or great art, whether it be a nude painting or a statue of a man or woman, it represents them in their natural state, in all the glory of their individual humanity. So-called Page 3 girls appeal to the lowest, basest instincts in men – the instinct to leer and feel superior to women, to keep them in the place they want them, ie as sexual objects for their pleasure and nothing more; to be used and be rid of at whatever cost.

TOWN WITHHELD

PEOPLE WHO THINK these pictures are harmless fun have got to be mindless morons, and as for Mr Bruinvel's* statement that there is freedom of choice – there is no freedom for millions of women who only just tolerate the papers their husbands bring home.

BELFAST

* Peter Bruinvels, MP for Leicester East, said 'Page 3 brightens up the day. I'm sure wives don't mind.' *The Sun*, 26 March 1986.

I AM NOT, as a rule, in favour of censorship, but I strongly support this Bill because for too long women have had to tolerate the attitudes such displays encourage. The idea that Page 3 is 'harmless' must be rejected. We are all aware of the 'power of the press' and *The Sun* persistently publishes sensationalised 'sex crime' stories alongside the pin-up. If violence against women is to be remedied, then Page 3 is the place to start. It would change my life knowing that millions of 'men on the street' were not digesting sex *and* violence before lunchtime.

LONDON

IT IS TYPICAL that Mr Adley equates the removal of such displays with a removal of individual rights. Of course, what he is talking about are the rights of dirty old men to gloat in the most disgusting fashion over the female form. What of the rights of women, the majority of the population, to be protected from the kind of acts which these displays may well provoke?

NORTHERN IRELAND

SUCH A LAW would infringe the rights of the individual? What individuals? Not women certainly, who would like the right – as individuals – to be regarded as autonomous, independent human beings; not there to be sniggered at, considered inferior and to only have an existence dependent on a man's view. It is a fact of life that if you give 'rights' to some people you disregard other peoples' rights. I think women have had their rights disregarded for too long.

TOWN WITHHELD

I'M FED UP of hearing the Freedom of Choice argument; don't they realise their so-called Freedom is our oppression?

DEVON

Index